RISE OF THE
REAPERS

AN INTERN DIARIES NOVELLA

BY D. C. GOMEZ

D . C . G O M E Z

ISBN: 978-1-7333160-3-3
Published by Gomez Expeditions
Request to publish work from this book should be sent to:
author@dcgomez-author.com

Other Books by D. C. Gomez

Urban Fantasy/ Young Adult:
Death's Intern- Book 1 in the Intern Diaries Series
Plague Unleashed- Book 2 in the Intern Diaries Series
Forbidden War- Book 3 in the Intern Diaries Series
Unstoppable Famine- Book 4 in the Intern Diaries Series

~

The Origins of Constantine- an Intern Diary Novella
From Eugene with Love- an Intern Diary Novella

Second Chance Romance/ Romantic Comedy:
The Cat Lady Special

Middle School Novel:
Another World- Book 1

And a children's series - Charlie's Fable
Charlie, what's your talent? - Book 1
Charlie, dare to dream! – Book 2

TABLE OF CONTENTS

RISE OF THE REAPERS...1
COPYRIGHT..2
OTHER BOOKS BY D. C. GOMEZ..3
TABLE OF CONTENTS...5
DEDICATION..6
CHAPTER ONE..7
CHAPTER TWO..11
CHAPTER THREE..16
CHAPTER FOUR...20
CHAPTER FIVE...26
CHAPTER SIX...30
CHAPTER SEVEN..35
CHAPTER EIGHT..41
CHAPTER NINE..47
CHAPTER TEN..53
CHAPTER ELEVEN..58
CHAPTER TWELVE...64
CHAPTER THIRTEEN..70
CHAPTER FOURTEEN..76
CONNECT WITH D.C...79
ACKNOWLEDGEMENTS...80
ABOUT THE AUTHOR..81

D.C. GOMEZ

For all of Constantine's fans,
Thank you for always believing.

CHAPTER ONE

PRESENT DAY- TEXARKANA TX

It was a warm winter, even for Northeast Texas. The trees were bare but winter refused to make its appearance. The Christmas decorations looked out of place next to the kids in shorts. The city of Texarkana, Texas had a twin city on the Arkansas side. In both cities, the people acted differently this winter than previous ones. It wasn't the weather affecting the residents; Constantine could feel the unrest in the air. After five-thousand years living around humans, the feline was very in tune with their mannerisms and traits.

When the cities of Texarkana became the official Haven for all supernatural beings in North America, the population in the cities doubled. The increased number of supernatural beings was slowly changing the dynamics of the cities. The human mind was incredible. It refused to process anything that it didn't understand. While the eyes registered the strange beings, the brain ignored it or blocked it. It was the only way the gnomes, pixies, fairies, shapeshifters, and all the other creatures were going unnoticed in the cities.

The Chamber of Commerce for the cities described the phenomenon as an economic boom. Businesses were moving into town and new residents were coming at an incredible rate. The cities were both expanding, which was a celebration for both communities. Unfortunately, the new residents brought with them their own set of problems that only Death's team could handle. It was due to Death's North American Intern, Isis Black, claiming Texarkana as her home that made the cities Haven. Policing the supernatural community was another duty that fell on their lists of things to do.

"At this rate, we will still be wearing shorts at Christmas," Bob told Constantine as he stared out the window of his baby blue truck.

"I'm sure the kids won't mind." Constantine licked his paw

and looked out the passenger window towards Whataburger's parking lot.

"That's just wrong." Bob shifted in his seat and carefully adjusted the gun in his pants holster.

"Why do you care? You hate Christmas. Last time I checked, you despise the cold and the snow." Constantine eyed Bob before returning to washing his face with his paw.

Constantine's cleaning habits were the only normal cat things Constantine ever did. He was an Egyptian cat who served as the guardian of the interns and Death's representative in the mortal world.

"It's about the principle of the matter," Bob answered, not making eye contact with his boss.

"Of course. Principles," Constantine replied rolling his eyes. "Let's make sure those principles don't get you killed."

A smirk spread across Bob's face as he ran his hand through his short blond hair.

"Do you think they will come?" Bob asked after a few minutes of silence.

Constantine took a few deep breaths. His fur radiated with a soft glow as he scanned the area like a true predator.

"Unfortunately, yes," Constantine answered. "Where else are they going to find this concentration of kids on a Friday night? It's not like we are in Dallas, or even a large metropolis."

"Great." Bob shook his head. "We don't need another werewolf gang in town?"

"Does anybody need a werewolf gang recruiting in their town?" Constantine snapped his head back. "Shorty is coming."

From his side mirror, Bob saw Shorty marching towards the truck. Like his name implied, Shorty was barely five-feet-four inches tall and maybe one-hundred and twenty pounds fully clothed. Shorty was hired by Constantine earlier in the year for his great network of connections in the town. Once a homeless man like Bob, Shorty now ran the most organized underground network of informants in the four-state region.

"Big Bob. Boss man." Shorty handed Bob a large strawberry milkshake.

"Anything out of the ordinary?" Bob asked as he poured the milkshake into a small ceramic bowl and placed it in front of Constantine.

"It's Friday night on New Boston Road, so everything is out of the ordinary." Shorty pointed across the street towards the auto parts store. "We found three kids high on pixie dust twenty minutes ago. The Triplets rushed them to the station. When I find that dealer, I'm going to choke him."

"Welcome to Haven," Constantine told both men in between licks of his milkshake. "Keep us posted."

"Will do." Shorty saluted Constantine and made his way across the street.

"Havens are a blessing and a curse," Constantine mumbled. "Everyone is always welcome. A blessing for everyone who is persecuted. Unfortunately, you always have those who take advantage of any opportunity. If we don't take full control of the situation, Texarkana could easily become a living hell."

Bob froze, holding his cup midair. "Hell? How?"

"With all the magic here, the death toll will quadruple." Constantine's gaze was distant. "Death will be busy escorting souls to their final destinations from this town at an astronomical rate."

"How do we stop that from happening?" Bob lowered his cup, unable to take another sip.

"Simple. They have to fear us more than the opportunities to make money or gain power." Constantine gave Bob a wicked grin, making his sharp canines shine in the night.

"I hope Isis is ready." Bob leaned his head against his window and looked down at his boss.

"Trust me. Give her two months of mediating supernatural domestic disputes and she will be ready." Constantine giggled. "That girl has a temper. You push her hard enough, and the goblins, trolls, and ghouls would be terrified of her."

"I hope you are right, boss," Bob replied, rubbing his eyes. "We might as well get comfortable. Looks like this could be a long night."

Constantine took his favorite Sphinx pose and watched the parking lot from his window. After a few minutes, he said, "Have I told you the story of how the Reapers were created?"

"I don't think so." Bob sat up in his seat and gave Constantine his undivided attention.

"This is a long one, but we do have plenty of time," Constantine said, starting his story. "We are not proud of this part of our history, but it happened. The year was four hundred and seventy-five AD, before the fall of the Roman Empire."

CHAPTER TWO

475 AD- ROME, ITALY

The narrow alley was dark, and the stench of human feces assaulted Constantine senses. The Romans claimed the Western Empire was the crown glory of the world, but Constantine usually disagreed. He never remembered ancient Egypt smelling this bad. The Roman Empire was in a state of turmoil, mainly because the young Emperor Romulus Augustus struggled to keep control of the empire while the wealthy were too busy enjoying their riches.

"This way Sergius. We don't have a lot of time." Constantine hurried down the alley towards a dark lump on the ground.

"Why do we always have to wander the city at night?" Sergius pulled on his toga and rushed quickly behind Constantine.

"Do you want to lose another soul?" Constantine muttered, stopping in front of the hump. "This one is fresh."

"Of course I don't, but some of us don't have your eyesight," Sergius replied, a little out of breath.

Sergius leaned down and turned the dismantled body around. The corpse had well-defined muscles, but the left side of his face and neck were gashed open. Constantine moved to the opposite side of the body and sniffed the corpse's clothing. Very little blood was found around the body despite the large wound on the neck.

Sergius leaned back on the balls of his feet, playing with his curly brown hair. On normal days, Sergius looked younger than his eighteen years, a great asset to help him fool the authorities and escape some very indiscreet situations. This evening, though, he looked aged and worried.

"Nothing. The soul is gone and I can't feel its presence anywhere around here." Sergius scanned the alley. "How is that possible? This man is still warm."

"Quiet." Constantine spun to face the entrance of the alley. "Hurry, someone is coming."

Sergius squinted, his eyes following the direction Constantine had been looking. Constantine jumped over the body and dragged Sergius by his tunic. They barely made it to the far corner when two large men walked toward the corpse. Sergius held his breath and Constantine stood ready to pounce.

"We need to assign this job to the new recruits," the taller of the two men said in a hushed voice.

"I wish," his companion replied, looking up and down the alley. "Last time that happened, those halfwits ate the body. Who eats flesh?"

The first man made a retching sound. "These new recruits leave a lot to be desired."

"Tell me about it. Grab the body; we have a lot to do. This day is not over." The second man headed out of the alley without waiting for a reply.

His companion picked up the body with one hand and tossed it over his shoulder in one smooth motion. He left the alley at a leisurely pace, like a man without a care in the world.

"Constantine, what in Christ's name is going on here?" Sergius moved slowly to the center of the alley. "There is no way they were able to see him from over there."

"Even if their vision wasn't extraordinary, they didn't need to see him. They knew exactly where to find him." Constantine moved, stopping next to Sergius. "This just confirms we have bigger problems than those two."

"We have bigger problems than men with superhuman strength that can see in the dark?" Sergius asked, his tone sarcastic as he paced circles around the location of their missing victim.

"If they were the only ones, I wouldn't care, but by the sound of their conversation, there are many more." Constantine smelled the ground, his ears twitching.

"What exactly do we have more of?" Sergius kneeled next to Constantine.

"Vampires," Constantine hissed the word. "A large concentration of them by the sound of their conversation."

"In Rome? That's impossible. We have an agreement." Sergius ran his hands over his hair, making it stand up straight. Sergius took a deep breath before speaking, but the veins on his forehead were pulsating. "What are we going to do?"

"We have to call Death." Constantine stood on all fours and

shook himself.

"I thought we were never supposed to call Death?" Sergius' voice cracked and sweat beads ran down his forehead.

"We? That sounds like too many people," Constantine replied, wiping his face with his paw. "You are not supposed to call Death. I can call whenever I want to. We need to leave before someone else comes to investigate."

Sergius followed Constantine out of the alley, looking over his shoulder. He adjusted his toga several times and picked up speed as soon as they cleared the alley.

Constantine and Sergius lived in a modest brick cottage by the Tiber River. The cottage was comfortable and secure but not so extravagant it would draw attention. Being employed by Death had provided Sergius with an increase in wealth, something he was still trying to get used to since he'd been a poor farm boy from the countryside. Constantine had advised not sharing his new occupation or income with anyone. The Roman Empire was in a transition of faith and accidentally informing one of the zealots could land them both in a dungeon.

While the cottage had very few neighbors, both Sergius and Constantine made it a point to avoid attention. They entered their residence through the back to avoid potential onlookers of their constant travels. As they entered the house, Sergius stopped short at the doorway. In the living room, he found a couple of candles lit.

"What are you doing?" Constantine asked after slamming into the back of Sergius legs.

"Somebody is here," Sergius whispered.

"Of course somebody is here. I told you I was calling Death." Constantine rolled his eyes and walked around Sergius towards the living room.

On the far side of the room, standing by a window stood Death. His muscular frame made him look dignified. He was wearing a Shendyt, an Egyptian male pleated skirt. His dark hair was combed back, making it sparkle when the light hit it.

"Well I see someone was home recently," Constantine told Death as he entered the room. "For a being who swore never to go back, you do spend a lot of time in that part of the world."

"People die everywhere, remember." Death never turned around to address Constantine. "What is so important that you dragged me here at this hour?"

"Your favorite pests of the realm are back." Constantine hopped on the small table in the center of the room and proceeded to clean the underside of his leg.

"Are you sure?" Death asked.

"We found eight dead bodies in the last three days but not a single soul," Constantine answered, not bothering to look up at his boss.

"Did any of the bodies have anything in common?" Death paced the room, staring at the floor.

"Nothing," Sergius answered from the door way.

"Oh, thank you for deciding to join the party." Constantine signaled to Sergius with his paw. "Would you care to come in or are you planning to hold that door up all night?"

"Sorry," Sergius mumbled.

"Death, you remember our little apprentice Sergius?" Constantine asked in an overly dramatic tone, pointing at Sergius.

"Don't be ridiculous. I know Sergius." Death shook his head and stopped pacing.

"Just making sure, since you come around so rarely. I figured introductions were in order." Constantine blinked fast and a mocking smile spread across his lips.

"Thank you for the reminder, but can we get back to your vampire theory." Death sat on one of the chairs and pointed to the empty one next to him. Sergius quickly took the seat.

"The rumors started at the capital after sightings of mysterious bodies that appeared and were gone by the time the legionnaires showed up." Sergius delivered his speech without breathing. "The strangest part was nobody came forth to report anyone missing. The witnesses swore the bodies they saw were dead but there is no proof."

"Tonight we saw two bloodsuckers collecting one of the bodies." Constantine cleaned his face as he spoke. "Have you heard anything in your travels?"

"Nothing." Death was rigid, his only movement coming from his index finger casually tapping his leg. "It seems like you two have work to do. We had an agreement and I want to know if the vampires have broken it. If they are taking humans without their consent, they will meet their end in the underworld."

"Yes, Death." Sergius bounced to his feet and saluted Death.

"I like him," Death told Constantine. "You could learn a few lessons from him."

"Not in this lifetime." Constantine hissed and rolled over, pointing his butt towards Death.

"Enough games Constantine. Get to work." Death snapped his fingers and disappeared.

"Wow, impressive," Sergius squealed.

"He is Death. Dramatic is part of his persona." Constantine rolled back to his side and sat up. "Unfortunately, he seems to be getting a little more arrogant with age. I hope that doesn't come back to get us."

"How do you get used to all his finger snapping and disappearing?"

"After a few millenniums, you don't even notice, but enough about Death. He is right, and we have a lot of work to do." Constantine slid down off the table, landing gracefully on the floor. "I have a few places to visit tonight, so get some rest. Tomorrow is going to be an early day."

"You don't want me to come with you?" Sergius asked as he sat down.

"Don't give me that lost puppy look," Constantine told Sergius.

"I'm not doing anything." Sergius pouted his lips and made his eyes wide and innocent.

"Of course not." Constantine glared at him. "Where I'm going, you won't fit. Go to sleep. You will have plenty to do tomorrow."

Before Sergius could say anything, Constantine jumped out of the open window. Sergius ran to the window, but Constantine had already disappeared.

CHAPTER THREE

Constantine and Sergius prowled the city before dawn. They avoided the stares of onlookers by staying on the deserted streets before sunrise. They made their way past the colosseum and arrived at the Market of Trajan. Trajan was a work of art. Five stories high and housing over one-hundred and fifty vendors, artisans, and business people, the market was a jewel to the Romans who loved to shop. Constantine had one special vendor in mind and they made their way as quickly as possible to the booth.

"Grab that basket." Constantine pushed a discarded basket at Sergius as they walked up the stairs.

"What exactly am I carrying in this thing?" Sergius asked, pulling the basket up.

Constantine leap inside. "Me. We don't need to draw any unnecessary attention. I'm too recognizable in these parts."

"And too humble by the looks of it." Sergius threw the basket over his shoulder and made his way up the market.

"Remember, we are looking for Marie," Constantine whispered from the basket.

"If you are trying to avoid drawing attention, not talking would be a great help," Sergius replied, keeping his face down while examining the vendors out of his peripheral vision.

The vendors were busy setting up for the day. Nobody paid any attention to Sergius or his talking basket. They climbed all the stairs and headed towards the far side of the fifth floor where the most affordable vendors were located. None of the wealthy patrons of Rome, or their slaves, ventured to that area. That was left for the poor citizens of the empire. By a wide window, a beautiful maiden organized breads, fruits, and jams.

"Your beauty illuminates this entire hallway," Sergius announced as he reached the young lady and her merchandise.

"The words just flow from your tongue like honey. What do I owe the pleasure of your visit, Sergius? And are you alone?" The maiden's eyes flicked every direction around Sergius.

"Of course not. He would never make it back from courting every pretty girl he sees." Constantine jumped out of the basket and strolled towards the young lady.

"That I do believe," she replied, crouching to rub Constantine's head.

"I don't court every girl I see. You are special, Marie," Sergius replied with his hand over his heart.

"Whatever you say, Sergius." Marie laughed softly. "What is the real reason you two are here? Something must be going on for both of you to be here before sunrise."

"Why do you have to assume something is wrong? Maybe I just can't stay away." Sergius dropped to one knee and grabbed the young lady's hand.

"Because she is right and we are wasting time." Constantine slapped Sergius over the head and leaped on the windowsill. "Marie, we need information, and it's urgent."

Marie pulled away from Sergius and sat next to Constantine by the window. Sergius stood up and joined them both, wiping his hands on his tunic.

"I'm listening." Marie peered down the hallway before talking. "Keep your voices low. You don't want everyone here listening."

"Have you heard anything about bloodsuckers?" Sergius whispered to her.

"Shh." Marie pulled Sergius to her and covered his mouth. "Definitely do not talk about that in here."

"What do you know?" Constantine inched closer to Marie.

Marie looked a little pale, and she chewed her bottom lip, then she squeezed her skirt tightly.

"Marie, what is going on?" Sergius asked, trying to make eye contact with the young lady.

"It started a few weeks ago. A couple of men came around questioning the vendors." Marie looked down at the ground, trying to catch her breath.

"What were they asking?" Constantine prodded her to continue.

"At first it was all innocent. How we felt about the empire and if we were happy with our faith." Marie's voice became softer and Sergius had to lean in to listen.

"Did they say anything that made you uncomfortable?" Constantine asked in a gentle tone. "Breathe Marie and just tell us."

"The questions always sounded normal and conversational, but they only spoke to the young man." Marie pointed to an empty space near her booth. "Last time I saw Titus, he was speaking with one of those men. Titus told me they had offered him an opportunity to join a prestigious group to serve the empire. Titus refused. He never came back to the market after that visit."

"How long ago was that?" Sergius asked, walking over to the vendors' empty space.

"Six days ago." Marie covered her sobbing face with her hands and wiped her cheeks. "What is happening?

"That's exactly what we are trying to find out," Constantine told her, rubbing his head on her shoulder. "Anything else you can tell us?"

"People have been leaving the market. The strangers come over and talk to the vendors. Some take the offer and leave their shops. Anyone who declines goes missing the next day." Marie wiped her face with her hands.

"Please don't cry. It is going to be fine." Sergius walked over to Marie and kneeled in front of her. Taking her hands, he peppered her hands with soft kisses.

"I'm going to be sick," Constantine mumbled while making choking sounds. "Marie, be careful and avoid any type of conversations about this topic. Sergius, we need to go. It is time we get to the bottom of this."

"Marie, promise me you will be careful." Sergius held her hand tightly.

"I will, as long as you stop overreacting." Marie pulled her hands away from Sergius, and before she stood, she kissed his forehead. "I'll be fine, I promise."

Constantine glanced at her one last time before he left the market with Sergius.

PRESENT DAY- TEXARKANA, TX

Bob leaned down closer to Constantine, listening attentively. More cars had arrived at the Whataburger, making the drive-thru line at least ten cars long.

"We should have never left her alone." Constantine faced the parking lot.

"You never saw her again?" Bob's sea-green eyes were wide and his mouth hanging open.

"That was the last time we saw her as a human." Constantine turned to face Bob. "There are many things I regret about that era. Her loss is one of the greatest. I can see the error in our actions now. We had so little information and gravely underestimated our enemy gravely."

"Boss, what…" Bob stopped himself as he followed a group of teenagers with his gaze as they approached a small Honda. "Are those our werewolves?"

Constantine lowered his window and focused on the group, sniffing the air for several seconds. Bob waited quietly for further instructions.

"I wish, but no." Constantine watched as the nine youths squeezed themselves inside the small four-door car.

"Do I want to know how they managed to get everyone in that car?" Bob asked Constantine, and the cat shook his head.

"Three witches, an elf, a shapeshifter, a pixies, and three humans, which is also the beginning of a horrible joke." Constantine stretched himself in the seat before getting comfortable again. "Trust me, you do not want to know how they all got in."

"They had a shifter in that group?" Bob took a sip from his shake and watched the car drive away. The amount of weight was making the back fender scrape against the ground. "How many more species are we expecting to join us in this little Haven?"

"Those are only the beginning. Soon, the wealthy ones will start moving in, so we better get things under control before that happens. Last thing we need is spoiled kids with money running the street." Constantine smoothed the fur on his stomach with his paw and turned back to watch the other cars in the drive-thru line.

"Boss, what happened to Marie?" Bob asked.

"It happened when we were away. I'm still not sure if she was taken, or she volunteered," Constantine resumed. "Sergius and I were having horrible luck in Rome getting any answers. Nobody wanted to talk to us. We took drastic measures and left the city. I still question if we should have taken Marie with us when we left."

CHAPTER FOUR

475 AD- ISLAND OF CAPRI

The deep blue water splattered against the tall cliffs. The island was breathtaking but only accessible by boat. Back in 27 AD, Emperor Tiberius had picked the island, both for its beauty and its strategic location. The cliffs were dangerous to scale, with jagged edges and deadly rock formations. The main road leading to the palace was heavily guarded by legionnaires.

"What are we doing here? You are not thinking of invading the palace?" Sergius asked Constantine over his shoulder.

Sergius had created a pouch with one of his tunics and placed Constantine inside. Supporting himself and Constantine proved to be challenging, but he was doing it.

"Have you lost your mind? That's a worthless suicide mission," Constantine replied in Sergius' ear. "There! That cave to your right is where we are going."

"How did you see that?" Sergius angled his body towards the cave and continued his climb.

"Unless you know where it is, you would never find it." Constantine leaped out of the tunic to a small ledge formed by rocks.

"You couldn't find an easier way to get here? I climbed all morning." Sergius pulled himself up the ledge and sat next to Constantine, breathing heavily. "By the way, you really need to lose some weight. You are a lot heavier than you look."

"Boy, I'm solid muscle." Constantine admired his physique, then stretched his limber body flat on the ground. "To answer your question, there is no way to get to the cave from the outside. The only other way is through the Grotta Azzura, and everyone who has tried to navigate that cavern has drowned. Figured you would rather face your chances on the cliffs."

"Those were our only options?" Sergius wiped the sweat from his face. "I hope this person is worth all this trouble. I'm tired already."

"She is worth it, trust me. Now come along." Constantine led the way on a thin passage towards the mouth of the cave. Before entering the cave, Constantine whispered to Sergius, "Whatever you do, don't touch anything."

Sergius only nodded and followed Constantine inside. The entrance to the cave was dark, and it reeked worse than the fish market. Sergius' steps made low crunching sounds while Constantine's were completely silent. Sergius looked down at the ground but the place was too dark to see anything. Deep inside the cave, a small candle was lit.

"I think it was better without any light since I know what's on the ground now." Sergius covered his nose and took shallow breaths. "Please tell me those are not human bones?"

"Not all of them." Constantine made his way towards a large cauldron near the light.

The ground was littered with bones of all shapes and sizes. Herbs in a variety of colors hung from hooks on both walls of the cave. A small table that looked more like an altar was placed next to the empty wall.

"Where is this person you are looking for?" Sergius asked, staying a few feet behind Constantine.

"Right behind you," a raspy voice whispered in Sergius' ear.

Sergius screamed, but before he could move, a knife dug into his neck, making him freeze and Constantine turn around, almost as if in slow motion.

"Balbinus! There you are, my favorite demented witch." Constantine smiled, and the light made his canines glow. "Put the knife down before you hurt someone. If you kill him, I will be forced to rip out your throat, and that would be a pity."

"Isn't that a lovely offer?" Balbinus pressed the knife harder to Sergius' neck. "Why are you here? Don't tell me you missed me."

"I have a job offer," Constantine said, stalking towards the witch.

"Sorry, I'm not looking for work. How about you and your frail little friend leave now?" Balbinus pushed Sergius towards Constantine.

"I'm not frail!" Sergius whined.

Balbinus made her way to the opposite side of the cauldron away from Constantine and Sergius. She wore a long, wool robe

with the hood hanging over her face. Even though it was dingy and
tattered, it covered her entire face and body, making it difficult to see
any of her features.

"You are pretty small compared to most soldiers."
Constantine inspected Sergius, his eyes moving up and down his
body.

"In that case it's a blessing I'm not a soldier." Sergius
crossed his hands over his chest and stuck his tongue out at
Constantine.

"Are you two done with your couple's quarrel?" Balbinus
pointed to the entrance of the cave with her knife. "Leave."

"We need your eyes." Constantine looked at the witch from
across the room. "We are not leaving until you help us."

Constantine strolled to the corner of the cave and made
himself comfortable on a pile of furs. Sergius followed Constantine
but kept looking over his shoulder every other step so he had an eye
on the witch.

"You are insufferable Constantine. Ugh!" Balbinus grabbed a
few herbs and mashed them with her fingers.

"Vampires are back to their old ways and we need to find
them." Constantine causally licked his paw.

"Are you sure?" Balbinus froze and stared at Constantine.

"We tracked them all over Rome for the last two months, but
we were always too late," Sergius volunteered.

"Why didn't you say that in the beginning?" Balbinus ripped
off her robe and got to work, gathering herbs, bones and other
ingredients from the cave in a rush.

"Wow, you are gorgeous." Sergius drooled at the sight of
Balbinus.

Balbinus was a tall, slender beauty in her early twenties. Her
golden hair looked as if it was made of silk, and the braid she wore
tightly behind her head seemed to go on forever. The thin white
tunic she wore barely covered her curves. Balbinus had one golden
eye and one blue eye, but instead of distracting from her beauty, it
only made her more mesmerizing.

"Yeah, yeah." Balbinus dismissed the compliment with a
wave of her hand. "I'm old enough to be your mother, boy. Do not
let this body deceive you?"

"Impossible." Sergius shook his head in disagreement. "You
are barely a few years older than me."

Balbinus laughed, the sound bouncing off the walls of the cave.

"Relax, my little hero." Constantine patted Sergius' leg. "Our little witch here is actually over two hundred years old. Trust her, she definitely could be your mother, grandmother, and almost any other of your predecessors.

"How is that possible?" Sergius observed the witch more carefully, and Balbinus gave him a flirty wink.

"I'm sure you don't have time to hear my little story." Balbinus circled the cauldron, mixing the ingredients with a large wooden spoon. "Do you have anything that belongs to those filthy creatures?"

Constantine motioned to Sergius, who pulled a small piece of cloth from his pocket. Sergius inched towards Balbinus, hesitant with his steps. When he tried to hand her the cloth, she refused to take it.

"Throw it in the cauldron. I don't need to contaminate it with my scent." Balbinus continued to stir the cauldron as Sergius dumped the cloth inside.

"How does it work?" Sergius asked, peering in the cauldron.

"I don't ask how you guys do your job, so don't question my methods." Balbinus slapped Sergius' hand away from her concoction. "I recommend you step away. It is going to get messy."

Sergius backed away until he stood next to Constantine, who climbed on the work bench and had a better look at the potion being brewed.

"What exactly are you looking for, Constantine?" Balbinus asked, her gaze not leaving her work.

"We need an address. After months of searching, all we have found is that piece of cloth you are boiling in there." Constantine leaned in closer, somehow maintaining his balance on the edge of the table.

"Can you really find them from just that piece?" Sergius peered into the cauldron.

"I can find anyone with less than that, so this will do nicely." Balbinus stirred the ingredients one more time. "Now quiet, I need to concentrate."

Balbinus raised both of her arms straight in the air. Her lips moved, but no sound came out. She swayed back and forth, and the liquid in the cauldron matched her rhythm. Her hands made small circles over her head and the brew mimicked her actions before it changed to a blood red color. Balbinus gave a small cry and her head dropped back.

"Oh God, should we help?" Sergius lunged forward but Constantine stopped him with one sharp claw.

"Don't touch her unless you want to end up in that pot," Constantine warned Sergius.

Balbinus slowly lifted her head. Her hair floated in an invisible wind, while her multicolor eyes were now black.

"That's not good." Sergius scurried back as far away from the possessed witch as he could get.

"The creatures for which you search are deep in your city." A harsh, cold male voice came out of the witch's mouth. "You will find the one you seek at this location."

Constantine leaned closer to the cauldron and looked at the image. A tavern full of people stood by a pier that overlooked a cliff.

"Thank you master. Your services have been most helpful." Constantine bowed to the witch, who licked her lips. "Sergius, please pay the master."

Constantine poked Sergius on the side to bring him back from his trance. Sergius pulled a small pouch from his tunic and dropped it in the corner where Constantine was pointing. A few gold coins escaped the pouch, but neither one bothered to retrieve them. The image in the cauldron slowly blurred away, and Balbinus dropped her head to her chest.

"Are you back Balbi?" Constantine purred to the witch.

"I hate when you call me that," she hissed. "I hope you found what you needed."

"Fisherman's Inn in Naples," Constantine replied.

"You figured that out from that image?" Sergius asked, looking between Constantine and the empty cauldron.

"Constantine has a perfect memory, little one, and he never forgets a single place, or person for that matter. Isn't that right, dear?" Balbinus asked, picking up the bag of coins.

"Tools of the trade," Constantine replied. "Thank you for your service, but we better be going."

"Kill them all, Constantine," Balbinus told him.

"That's the plan." Constantine headed out of the cave, followed by Sergius.

Outside of the cave, Sergius asked, "Why does she hate them

so much?"

"Vampires turned her only brother against his will. Balbinus had to kill him before he killed their family," Constantine answered, searching the ledge of the cliff. "Balbinus hunted that vampire for decades, but too many people had been converted to vampires in her village. Her family was butchered while she was hunting."

"That is awful." Sergius glanced back towards the cave.

"She takes pleasure in eliminating vampires whenever she can, which is the reason she helped us," Constantine added.

"What are you expecting to find at this inn?" Sergius asked as he stretched his legs.

"Anything," Constantine admitted. "Right now, all we have are dead leads, no pun intended.

"A fresh one would be nice." Sergius looked down the cliff at the sharp rocks below. "Guess we are climbing down?"

"Not this time." Constantine pointed to a pile of furs. "We are sliding down."

Sergius walked over to the furs and found a long rope underneath. Sergius smiled at Constantine as he dropped the rope down the side.

"I like going down much better than up." Sergius grabbed Constantine and placed him in the back of his tunic.

Without another word, Sergius repelled down the side of the cliff and towards their boat.

CHAPTER FIVE

The port of Naples had as much traffic as any of the major ports in the empire. Vessels were constantly entering and leaving the city. Many boats carried legionnaires or supplies to many locations across the land. Stories of unrest and civil wars were escalating, and in return, the empire sent more troops to many of the major cities and ports. Constantine and Sergius paid for passage to Naples from a fisherman near Rome. They hoped to avoid dictation from the vampires by blending in with the regular population. The fisherman was eager to agree. He had a horrible season due to the high winds and deadly storms. At least he would return home with money in his pocket just by bringing a strange young man with an angry cat.

Constantine and Sergius arrived at the port late in the afternoon but didn't leave the boat until the middle of the night. The least amount of people knowing of their arrival the better. The plan was to gather as much information as possible on their enemies and return to Rome to prepare a plan. Fortunately for the two friends, Fishermen's Inn was a short walk from the port, and Constantine led the way through dark alleys and rat infested side streets.

"I was under the impression Naples was a magnificent city." Sergius scurried around a rat the size of a small rabbit.

"Naples is a beautiful city, but not this part." Constantine swatted a few rats that refused to move out of his way. "This is where men fall prey to sins of the flesh, as your dearly departed apostle called it."

"Did you meet any of the apostles?" Sergius asked as they scurried across the alley to the back of a two-story building.

"Yes, a few." Constantine looked up and down the street. "I admired their commitment and focus, even though they all knew it was a suicide mission. But that's a tale for another time."

"Why am I not surprised you knew them?" Sergius told Constantine.

"I have been around for a long time and have met a lot of people. Now is not the time to discuss that, though. Stay focused." Constantine motioned towards the building next to them. "This is the building. You are listening for information. Don't ask too many questions."

"Got it." Sergius adjusted his tunic and headed inside the Fishermen's Inn.

The main floor of the Inn was a large tavern. Wooden tables littered the room but few patrons were still around. Sergius walked slowly towards the back of the room, keeping his head low and breathing steady. He found a small table in a corner and sat down.

"What can I get you?" a young maiden asked with a wide, toothy smile. She was curvaceous with curly red hair. Her face was average, but her other assets made up for that, attracting the attention of the patrons.

"A large Calda if you still have it," Sergius answered casually while looking around the tavern.

"Not any more. All we have is Posca." The smile was gone from the Maiden's face as she waited for Sergius to reply.

"In that case, bring me two. If you have any bread and fruits, could you bring that out as well?" This time Sergius gave her his undivided attention and placed two gold denarius Aureus in her hand.

"Of course master, as you wish." The maiden pocketed the coins and scurried back to the kitchen.

"That's a lot of money for a young fellow," a large man with a silver beard told Sergius from the next table. "These are dangerous times."

"Then it's a good thing I'm not traveling alone," Sergius replied, bowing his head to the stranger. "Our master sent a group of us down to find entertainment for his upcoming party. I figured he wouldn't mind if I feed myself after doing all his dirty work."

"The patricians and their parties." The man spat on the ground in disgust. "They are the reason the empire is falling apart. They deserve what is coming to them."

"What is coming?" Sergius lowered his voice and looked directly at the man.

"You will see. It's only a matter of time." The man stood from his chair and his large frame almost touched the ceiling. "Enjoy the meal. Your master doesn't deserve your service."

Sergius observed the man as he exited the tavern. Two other patrons followed shortly after him. Only four people remained in the tavern, and that included Sergius. Two drunks laid motionless over their tables, while the remaining patron ate his food quietly.

"Here you go, master. Will you need anything else?" The maiden placed the glasses of wine in front of Sergius large enough for four people.

"Thank you, this will be enough." Sergius smiled. "Are you normally this slow?"

The maiden's gaze scanned the tavern, a nervous look passing over her face. "People are afraid to come out at night lately. You never know who you will find."

"I believe that." Sergius struggled to pick his glass up without spilling the drink

The maiden gave him another close-lipped smile and left his table. She made her way around the tavern, wiping down tables and picking up empty plates. Sergius finished his drink but ignored the rest of the food.

After an hour, the tavern remained empty. Sergius left quietly and headed straight to the alley where Constantine waited.

"That was a waste of our time," Sergius announced as he reached Constantine.

"But not for us." The two patrons that had left the tavern dropped down from the roof.

Sergius tried to scream but the tallest of the men slammed him to the wall, knocking the air out of his lungs. The duo moved with a quickness that made Sergius' head hurt. Sergius kicked and punched, but his assaults never landed. The duo laughed at his failed attempts. The first assailant picked Sergius up by the neck and pinned him to the wall.

"You will make a delicious meal for our master this evening." The man opened his mouth and his jaw stretched to a size that wasn't humanly possible. Canines and teeth appeared as large as sharks' teeth.

"Too bad he already has plans for the evening." Constantine pulled the vampire off Sergius.

Sergius dropped to the ground, wrapping his hand around his throat while trying to breathe, and when he glanced up, Constantine had turned into a large lion and was ripping the vampire apart. No blood flew anywhere, but the vampire turned to dust that dropped to the ground and flew through the air.

"I don't know what you are, but your friend here is going to die." The second vampire reached for Sergius.

Sergius rolled to his side and landed next to a pile of tools. He grabbed the closest one to him, a scythe, and scratched the incoming vampire across the chest. The vampire did not evaporate into dust, but the assault stopped his approach.

"This is not over," the vampire hissed and leaped over the building.

"Are you alive, Sergius?" the lion asked.

"Constantine, please tell me that is you?" Sergius watched as the lion shifted to a cat-sized Constantine.

"Wow that is incredible." Sergius leaned down to touch Constantine's fur. "How did you do that?"

"We don't have time to explain, and get your hands off me." Constantine slapped Sergius away, who was still trying to pet him. "Did you recognize those two?"

"No. They were in the tavern but left shortly after I arrived. I never learned who they work for but they looked normal." Sergius dropped to the ground and rested his head against the wall.

"They work for the Senator of this region. You didn't recognize them as vampires?" Constantine walked over to Sergius and peered at his face from inches away.

"What are you doing?" Sergius tried to back away, but he was pinned between Constantine and the wall.

"We have a problem. If you are not able to recognize them, you are as good as dead." Constantine hopped off Sergius and marched out of the alley. "What are you waiting for? Let's go."

"Besides being attacked, we didn't find anything." Sergius struggled to get to his feet.

"But we learned high members of the Senate have vampires as employees, and might even be vampires themselves. That alone is a lot of information. We need to hurry." Constantine rushed out of the alley. "A ship is leaving out of here before dawn, and we need to be in it. You should bring your new weapon. I have a feeling we are going to need it."

Sergius grabbed the scythe and ran out of the alley behind Constantine. He was limping a little but not enough to slow him down. Constantine did not waste any time hiding in alleys. Instead, he took the main road to the port and out of the treacherous sector.

CHAPTER SIX

The dim light of the candle in the living room was the only light in the house. Sergius and Constantine sat on opposite sides of the living room, each lost in their own thoughts. Rome was crawling with legionnaires, twice as many as normal. Unlike Naples, it appeared citizens were encouraged to be out at night. The streets were full of people and nobody seemed concerned with the current state of the empire.

Sergius and Constantine sprang to their feet at the sound of the backdoor being opened. Sergius pulled out of a knife from his toga. Constantine had ordered him to start carrying one for protection. Constantine's claws were fully extended. They each took a position on either side of the door, waiting for the intruders quietly.

"Hey, what is wrong with you two?" the young man screamed after being pushed to the wall by Sergius, and after Constantine bit his leg.

"Nico, what are you doing here?" Sergius let go of Nico and walked back to his seat.

"Constantine, do you mind letting go of my leg?" Nico looked down at Constantine, who was still latched on.

Constantine squeezed one last time and walked away as well. Nico followed them into the living room and took a seat.

"How did you know we were home?" Constantine lunged back on his seat and made himself comfortable.

"I have been coming around the house every night. I wasn't sure you would be home, but I was hoping." Nico took a deep breath and dropped his head against the back of the chair.

"What's happening?" Constantine asked.

"The city has gone mad," Sergius muttered.

"What else is new?" Constantine replied, not looking at Nico.

"They are looking for you two." Nico closed his eyes.

"Who?" Sergius jumped to his feet and pace the room.

"The legionnaires," Nico mumbled.

"That's unexpected. Why?" Constantine turned to look at Nico, his ears straight up.

"People are worried about all the questions you've been asking." Nico opened his eyes to focus on Constantine. "Nobody understands your business, but they are worried. To make things worse, people are saying that vampires have infiltrated the legions and are making decisions against their enemies."

"Now that makes sense," Constantine told both men.

"What part of that makes sense?" Sergius stopped pacing and walked towards Constantine.

"These vampires seem highly organized, well trained, and as if they have plenty of funds to run their operations. How else could they pull this off?" Constantine settled back in his chair and started his grooming ritual.

"That's not all." Nico faced Sergius. "Marie is missing. Nobody has seen her in three days."

"What?" Sergius rushed to Nico's side. "Tell me everything you know. What happened?"

"Sergius, please come down," Nico replied, his voice trembling. "Marie had been asking a lot of questions as well. She left the market for lunch and never came back. When I checked with her father, she never made it home."

"This is all my fault." Sergius was back to pacing the room, this time faster. "I told her to stay out of this. Why doesn't she ever listen?"

"Marie is just as stubborn as you are. She doesn't follow orders from anyone," Nico told Sergius from his chair.

"Our little friend has a point," Constantine told Sergius. "Once Marie sets her mind to something, nobody can stop her."

"Thanks Constantine but you are not helping." Sergius looked out the window. "We need to find her."

"Don't you dare leave this abode," Constantine growled at Sergius. "If Nico is correct, the city is crawling with legionnaires turned into vampires, and they are all looking for you. You stay here and I'll go looking for information."

"You can't expect me to do nothing?" Sergius' face was bright red and his nails were digging into his fists.

"I expect you to be smart about things." Constantine jumped down from the chair. "You are not going to find Marie or be of any use to her if you are dead. Start thinking and stop being emotional. Nico, anything else we should know?"

"Maybe, but this can't be true." Nico scratched his head before continuing.

"What can't be true?" Constantine hopped back on the living room table, looking Nico straight in the eyes.

"The rumors around town all mention that the bloodsuckers are working directly for the Emperor," Nico replied softly. "Some believe that the bloodsuckers are working as the Emperor's personal soldiers."

"This could complicate things." Constantine sat on his hind legs. "If they have access to the Emperor, their power and reach could be endless. Nico I need you back on the streets, let me know if you hear anything else."

"On my way Constantine." Nico saluted Constantine and ran out of the living room.

"Sergius, tomorrow morning, you need to get in touch with your contacts in the city," Constantine ordered. "We are going to need a lot more apprentices."

"Let me change these clothes and I'll be on my way as well." Sergius walked past Constantine as he headed towards his room.

Constantine grabbed Sergius by the leg with his claws. "Not in the middle of the night, foolish boy. Didn't you hear anything I said? I need you start doing that in the morning, while the sun is out."

"What difference is it going to make?" Sergius looked down at Constantine.

"It's bad enough having legionnaires looking for you, but adding vampires is a nightmare." Constantine let go of Sergius. "Try to sleep. I will go do some scouting tonight.

"How come you get to go out?" Sergius pouted and crossed his arms.

"Nobody is looking for a stray cat roaming the city. They are looking for a man and a cat. If we are separate, they are going to have a harder time finding us." Constantine smiled at Sergius. "I will take the night, and you do the day. We have to be smart here."

"I don't like it." Sergius dropped himself on the chair vacated by Nico. "Do you have a plan?"

"The two of us are not enough to take on an army of

vampires, and we need help," Constantine told Sergius.

"We are going to need a lot of help," Sergius agreed.

Constantine left the cottage to start his recruitment mission. He didn't trust Sergius to stay home and mind his own business. Not only did he have connections with many of the humans in the city, but he also knew every four-legged creature in Rome. He left a dozen stray cats watching the house, each in a different location. Their orders were simple: If Sergius left the house, they followed him. If anyone entered the house, they were to contact him immediate. Constantine couldn't watch Sergius all the time, but he could assign the work to very reliable sources for only a few fish. Paying felines for their services was a lot cheaper than humans.

With Sergius under surveillance, Constantine made his way to all his usual spots. He started with the innkeepers and tavern owners. He checked for any former soldier or slaves from any other countries who were looking for work. Their replies were always the same: Nobody was willing to risk their lives for a lost cause. The new comers to the city had heard rumors of the vampires' recruitment process and what happened to those that disagreed. Even those with nothing to lose were terrified to get involved. Fear was a great tool for control.

Constantine made one last stop to his favorite tavern on the fisherman's quarters. The owner, Horatio, was an old associates of Constantine's who still believed in freedom for people. They met in the alley behind the tavern, where Horatio sat on the ground next to Constantine, both with a glass of Horatio's finest wine.

"Constantine, you know I would join you in this. But these old bones wouldn't last a day in battle, not against those monsters." Horatio took a sip of his wine.

"I know, old friend, and I'm not asking you to join us. I just need to find some able bodies." Constantine dipped his claw in the glass and stirred the wine.

"You are only looking for able bodies?" Horatio asked.

"What do you mean?" Constantine glanced up at his friend.

"Normally you are looking for the cream of the crop, but if it's only able bodies you need, I might know where you can find some." Horatio winked at his friend and this time took a gulp of his wine.

"Am I going to like these men?" Constantine asked.

"They are good men, just rough, misunderstood, and not afraid to hold their ground. You offer them a nice wage and hot meals, and you, my friend, will have an army." Horatio looked around the rooftops of the nearby buildings. "You are going to need them Constantine. The bloodsuckers are multiplying rapidly, and because of the lack of control by the empire, the vampires are becoming bolder by the day."

"Where can I find them?" Constantine took a sip of his wine.

"A small tavern by the port is one of their normal spots. Just be careful my friend. You won't be the only one recruiting them." Horatio stood and headed inside the tavern.

Constantine took another lick from his glass before taking off. He watched the shadows move in the alley and realized he was being watched. If Constantine's only option to save humanity was to recruit a bunch of miscreants, then he better be quick about it before the shadows were able to close in. Sprinting down the alley, he moved as fast as a jaguar on a hunt. Not even vampires could keep up with him.

CHAPTER SEVEN

Constantine had spent most of the night talking to as many people as he could. He was passed out on the living room table by the time Sergius woke up. Sergius tip-toed to the table where Constantine was sleeping and leaned down.

"If you don't want to lose that hand, I wouldn't do that if I were you," Constantine hissed, his eyes still closed.

"You were snoring, so how could you possibly have heard me coming?" Sergius dropped into the chair next to Constantine, his bottom lip extended in a pout.

"Sergius, it isn't not your fault. I have extremely good hearing. To me, you sound like a small elephant moving through a glass shop." Constantine rolled over and stretched.

"Thank you for letting me down gently." Sergius joined Constantine, reaching his arms over his head and yawning. "Did you made it in last night?"

"Right before dawn, but it was a long night. I'm surprised you stayed in all night." Constantine turned to look at Sergius.

"Did you have people spy on me?" Sergius asked.

"Not people, but they did keep an eye on you for your safety." Constantine stood on the table and looked around the room.

"Of course it was for my safety. Any word on Marie?" Sergius pulled his legs up to his chest and took slow breaths.

"None. It's like the earth swallowed her whole. I have all four-legged spies searching the city," Constantine told him. "That's all we can do now. In the meantime, we have work. It's going to be another long night. We have a meeting this evening."

"Who are we meeting?" Sergius asked.

"A bunch of tough men who are willing to fight." Constantine smiled wickedly.

"Are they trustworthy?" Sergius started biting his nails, rocking back and forth.

"I have no idea, but we might not have a lot of choice here,"

Constantine replied. "If they join our cause, we will find out the true nature of their character."

"I hope you know what you are doing." Sergius looked around the room. "What do we do in the mean time?"

"Breakfast would be a great start." Constantine leap from the table. "We have a few visits to do before our meeting this evening."

"Guess we will start with breakfast then." Sergius followed Constantine out of the room and towards the kitchen.

It was a moonless night, and the darkness reached across the city like millions of hands grabbing everything. Sergius and Constantine crossed the streets of Rome on their way to the port. They avoided congested areas, staying close to the shadows. Sergius was busy looking over his shoulder, tripping over his own feet on several occasions. Constantine stayed low to the ground, moving quickly around corners and open areas. They arrived at a large building near the water. The front of the building was locked, so they entered the building from the back.

A small run-down door was ajar. Constantine went in first, slithering his way through the small space. Sergius waited by the door, keeping watch on the surrounding building.

"All clear," Constantine whispered to Sergius.

Without replying back, Sergius pushed his way inside and shut the door as much as he could. The inside of the building smelled of mildew. The only light in the room came from a small candle on top of a table in the center of the room. Sergius found Constantine underneath the table struggling to open a small box.

"Do you need help?" Sergius asked, kneeling next to Constantine.

"We need a few more candles. We don't want to scare away our potential army." Constantine pushed the box towards Sergius.

Sergius pulled the lid off the box and grabbed a handful of candles. He lit the candles and spread them around the room. The additional light made the room look less menacing. It was still not welcoming, but at least it looked functional. Constantine turned to face the door, ears fully extended.

"What is it?" Sergius turned in the same direction.

"Someone is coming." Constantine crawled toward the door.

"Constantine, we are here." Nico rushed towards the light, a young man with dark blond hair keeping pace with him.

"What are you two doing here?" Sergius asked first.

"That is a very good question." Constantine joined the trio.

"We are here to help," Nico announced. "Linus and I are experts in gathering information."

"That is great. Too bad we need fighters," Constantine told the young men who were beaming with joy.

"We don't have time for this. You two need to go before people get here." Sergius grabbed both Nico and Linus by the arm.

"Too late for that, Sergius. Our visitors are here." Constantine pointed in the opposite direction. "Everyone get behind the table and let me do the talking."

Sergius dragged Nico and Linus with him, while Constantine maneuvered himself on the table next to the candle and got comfortable. As he adjusted his tail, two large men came into view. They were over six feet tall with biceps bigger than a normal person's head. Constantine waited motionless as the men came nearer.

"This is a small crowd," one of the men with brown hair spoke first.

"You are early," Constantine replied softly. "But don't fear, a few more are right behind you."

The two men turned around to watch several more enter the building. The new arrivals were just as big as the first, with more muscles and weapons everywhere. In a short time, over thirty men gathered around Constantine, all the men looking at each other without talking.

"Not a bad turn out for such a short notice," Constantine announced. "Welcome to the party."

"I heard the rumors but didn't believe it." One of the men in the back shook his head. "A talking cat. Never thought I'd see the day."

"Did you also hear this cat can rip your throat apart if you betray him?" Constantine stood atop the table, claws fully extended and canines showing.

"They mentioned that, yes," another replied with a chuckle.

"We were promised a fortune if we join your little crew," a smaller man with thick brown hair stepped forward. "Is that true?"

"What's your name?" Constantine asked.

D . C . G O M E Z

"Julius," the man replied, facing Constantine.

"Julius, the pay is more than you will make in a year, but survival rate is low," Constantine told the crowd. "This job is not for everyone."

"Or you can join us and rule the world," a male spoke from behind the crowd.

The group turned to face the man, who was flanked by two others. The speaker was tall with jet black hair, a perfect complexion, and he wore an officer's uniforms. His companions had similar uniforms, but one had straight brown hair while his companion's hair was curly. Constantine stood at the edge of the table, ready to leap. Sergius covered his friends with his body.

"What makes you think we want to join the legion?" Julius asked, and the crowd laughed.

"Who said we are legionaries? Jet Black smiled at Julius, making sure his teeth were visible to the group. The group gasped as the fangs glistened in the light.

"What do you guys offer?" Julius asked, his voice no more than a soft whisper.

"Immortality, power, riches..." Jet Black answered.

"Death," Constantine interrupted him. "Don't forget death and damnation. And your soul will be lost for all eternity."

"Do I look dead to you?" Jet Black laughed at Constantine. "The talking cat offers you money, but I offer you the world."

"All you have to do is let them nibble on your neck, take your life, and you give up your free will forever," Constantine purred in a condescending tone.

The group of men turned to looked at the vampires, then their eyes fell on Constantine again.

"Yes, my friends, your will is part of the deal," Constantine clarified for the crowd. "You will forever have a master you report to and do his work. Good luck ruling the world."

"Or we just walk away," one of the men in the group said and marched towards the door.

"You will choose a side," Curly growled, stepping in front of the man.

The man pushed past the vampire, and the creature tossed the man five foot in the air and he landed against a wall. Half of the group pulled weapons from their togas and charged the three vampires. Within seconds, five men were dead, shredded to pieces, and the remaining were limping or missing appendages.

"Join us or prepare to die," Jet Black ordered the crowd.

"Oh, I hate when my guests are mistreated." With a swift swing of Sergius' scythe, Death cut Curly in half from behind.

The vampire erupted into dust as Death walked through it. The men pulled back, dragging their wounded with them. Jet Black and his friend faced Death, teeth bared and claws extended.

"You know the deal. You do not take a life without their permission." Death pointed the scythe at the two vampires.

"You are the famous Death? I was expecting something more frightening." Jet Black laughed.

"Who needs to be frightening when I will be the last thing you will ever see?" Death moved with lightning speed toward the vampires.

Before the vampires could move, Death ripped Jet Black's head off with his bare hands, and his companion was impaled to the ground with the scythe. Death casually wiped his hands off as the vampires disintegrated into dust.

"You are late," Constantine told Death as he sat back on the table.

"I had deliveries to make," Death replied. "Speaking of that, Sergius, would you please gather our friends over there. I will be with them shortly."

"Of course Death." Sergius ran towards the dead bodies.

The crowd watched silently. As Sergius approached one of the bodies, the man's ghost appeared.

"By the gods, what is this sorcery?" one of the men screamed.

"Oh please, it's your soul you fool," Constantine shouted back. "That's what you will be giving up to the vampires. When you die your second death, there will be nothing left but dust. They will be going home now."

Whispers and murmurs spread around the group. Some of the men's complexions changed to a light shade of green, while a few threw up on themselves.

"Unlike the vampires, we will not force you to join us." Death crossed the room and stood next to Constantine. "These are dangerous times, and you are free to choose. But if you choose their side, let me warn you, a war is coming. If you cross us, we will hunt you down."

"Can you offer us your abilities?" Julius stepped forward and asked. "We all saw it, and we are no match for those beasts this way. If you can't make us their equals, we are all as good as dead."

"That's an idea," Death replied, crossing his arms over his chest.

"When you decide, you let us know." Julius walked over to one of the dead and picked him up by the shoulder. "We have people to bury now. Please take care of their souls."

Without waiting for Death's response, the group picked up their dead and left the building. Sergius stood to the far side with the five souls. He spoke in soft voices with the dead as Death and Constantine watched.

"Are you sure you two want to join this?" Constantine asked Nico and Linus, who were huddled in the corner.

"War is coming whether we want it or not. I don't think we have a choice," Nico answered, wiping his tears with his sleeves.

"It's going to be a bloody one, Constantine, so we need to be ready," Death told his friend in a quiet voice. "I will meet you back at the cottage after I deliver these men."

Constantine nodded and watched Death take charge of the souls. He gathered them like lost sheep in the night. Constantine took a deep breath and sprang down from the table.

"We need to get back home," Constantine announced to the living. "I'm sure their master was watching that episode and more will be coming."

Death disappeared with the souls and Sergius joined Constantine, Linus, and Nico.

"Death said we need to hurry home," Sergius informed Constantine.

"I completely agree, so let's go." Constantine led the way out of the building as fast as the men could follow.

The three young men followed closely behind, occasionally looking over their shoulders. The streets were still dark, but the air felt sticky and humid. The group picked up their speed across the port.

CHAPTER EIGHT

Death was already in the living room when Constantine and Sergius walked in. Constantine was the first one to spot Death leaning against the window in the dark room as he held Sergius' scythe. Sergius lit a few candles while Constantine strolled over to Death.

"I thought we were over you moping around in corners," Constantine whispered to his old friend.

"Not moping this time. More like plotting." Death chuckled, still staring outside. "If I hadn't arrived, it would have been a massacre. They killed five of the toughest men in the city in less than a blink."

"But you made it," Constantine answered.

Death pushed himself away from the window, dragging the scythe with him. He leaned the weapon on one of the chairs and sat down. Sergius remained standing, while Constantine made himself comfortable across the table from Death.

"I hope you don't mind that I borrowed your scythe, Sergius," Death whispered.

"Not at all, it comes in handy," Sergius replied, fidgeting with his hands.

"War is imminent, now, and I can't be everywhere at all times." Death ran his hands through his hair. "Julius was right. If I can't make the humans as strong as the vampires, this is going to be a slaughter."

"I don't like where this is going." Constantine stood from his chair and hopped on the table to be closer to Death.

"What if we gave them selected powers?" Death faced Constantine before continuing. "Give them the strength, agility, and speed of vampires with my powers to kill them."

"Is that even possible?" Sergius asked, taking a seat in the chair Constantine had vacated.

"It has never been done before," Death replied.

"But is it safe?" Constantine asked.

"You survived." Death winked at Constantine.

"Not the same and you know it." Constantine rolled his eyes at Death. "We share a life force. You would be giving them unlimited powers with no constraint. Humans have a way of being power hungry and reckless. No offense Sergius."

"None taken. You are right." Sergius sucked in long breath. "Humans with that kind of power and without the limitation the vampires have could be extremely dangerous."

"Sounds like restrictions would be in order." Death stood from his chair and started pacing. "Long life but still able to die. That's the balance of nature."

"You are serious about this?" Constantine covered his face with his paws. "This could end badly."

"Our current situation is already bad. People are being changed all the time, most against their wishes. Others are just being killed. We need to stop them." Death halted his pacing to stare at Constantine.

"You have a point." Constantine resigned himself and sat on the table, shaking his head. "What's the plan?

"Guess we need to start making an army—an army of Reapers." Death slowly walked over to the chair and grabbed the scythe.

"Reapers?" Constantine looked behind him towards Sergius, who just shrugged.

"Yes, my friend. It's harvest season and we are going to rid the earth of all the bad seeds." Death spun the scythe in one hand, making the blade shine in the candlelight.

"You are so dramatic at times." Constantine shook his head.

"What do you need me to do?" Sergius asked Death, jumping up from his chair.

"You are not doing anything besides sitting back in that chair," Constantine growled at him.

"We need an army, and we don't even know if this superhuman thing is going to work," Sergius told both Constantine and Death, the words rushing from in. "We might as well try it with me. Last thing we need is to run the experiment in front of the crowd and have it go horribly wrong."

"Sergius, are you sure?" Death held Sergius by the shoulders. "Whatever happens, there is no turning back."

"No, but we are all eventually going to die." Sergius' voice cracked. "If I don't make it, I would like to see heaven. The apostles said it is an amazing place, even better than the Elysian Plains."

"I knew letting you follow the teachings of Paul was a bad idea." Constantine rolled his eyes.

"I will not force this on anyone. It has to be your free will." Death scanned Sergius' face carefully.

"It is my will to do this," Sergius replied softly.

"I don't like this," Constantine added.

"We don't have a lot of options here," Death replied, not looking at Constantine. "Take a deep breath Sergius, then close your eyes and clear your mind."

Sergius followed the orders, closing his eyes while taking a deep breath. Constantine moved to a chair closer to both men. Death placed both his hands on Sergius' face, covering his ears and temples, then he took a deep breath and slowly breathed out on Sergius.

"Anubis, are you sure?" Constantine whispered.

"I need to concentrate, Constantine, but yes, we must do this," Death snarled back.

White light covered Sergius from head to toe. Death chanted softly over him. The light changed colors from white to yellow to red as Death spoke to it. "Strength, speed, power, and immortality, this I give you."

Death let go of Sergius and the light sank into his skin. As the light receded, Sergius' body vibrated, then he screamed and dropped to the ground, writhing and screaming out in agonizing pain. Constantine jumped next to him but Death stopped him.

"Don't touch him." Death kneeled next to Sergius and watched the transformation. "I'm not sure how your powers would mix with his."

"Powers? He looks like he is being shredded from the inside out." Constantine stood, ready to pounce on Sergius as he rolled around on the ground.

The screams stopped then, and Sergius rolled into a ball on the ground, covered in sweat. Constantine and Death watched him from a few feet away. Sergius stirred, but he couldn't lift his head. Death grabbed the scythe and waited for Sergius to move, and Constantine extended his claws, prepared to attack. Sergius turned to face the duo, sweat matting his hair to his face. Slowly he wiped the sweat away, exposing silver irises.

"That's unexpected," Constantine told Death.

"Sergius, how do you feel?" Death asked, pointing the scythe at the young man.

"Like I've been stomped by a horse." Sergius' voice was scratchy and rough. "It hurts to talk."

"I just dumped a lot of power into you, you are going to need rest." Death moved closer to Sergius. "Can you stand?"

Sergius nodded and took Death's hand. Death examined him carefully as he helped him up. Sergius was dizzy but managed to stay standing.

"Wow, now that's impressive." Constantine whistled at Sergius.

Death looked down at Sergius' chest. The young man had developed well-defined muscles, both in his chest and arms. His legs were equally impressive with a physique that would mirror any gladiator.

"He has the muscles alright." Constantine walked around Sergius, inspecting his legs as well as his back. "Do you feel any different? Like you have a craving for blood?"

"Yes, that is important to know. Are you feeling a need to eat a human?" Death asked Sergius, holding on to his arm.

"I'm really thirsty but I'm sure it isn't for blood." Sergius tried to pull away from Death but fell backwards.

"Not the most intimidating move when you land on your butt." Constantine climbed on Sergius' lap and looked directly into his eyes. "Why did you agree to become Death's apprentice?

"What? Are you serious?" Sergius tried to stand up but Death pushed him back down.

"Answer the question, Sergius." Death held him in place as Constantine got closer to his face.

Sergius took a deep breath. "I never wanted anyone to die alone like my mother did. I wanted to help the souls find their way home in peace." Tears ran down Sergius face as he looked down at Constantine, who gently wiped them away with his paws.

"He is still there." Constantine bounced off Sergius with a smile. "You can put him to bed now."

"What?" Sergius whined as Death pulled him back up.

"I needed to make sure we hadn't lost your soul in this transformation." Constantine smiled wickedly. "You passed."

"Constantine. Sergius." Nico rushed in the room screaming at the top of his lungs.

"Boy, what is the matter? Didn't we leave you at your house?" Constantine reprimanded Nico.

"They took her and they want you at the port tomorrow or they are going to kill her," Nico rambled, not even taking a breath.

"Slow down Nico, we have no idea what you are talking about." Constantine moved back on the table to have a better look at Nico.

"The vampires took Marie," Nico replied, crying.

"Are you sure?" Sergius asked.

"By the Gods, what happened to you?" Nico moved closer to Sergius but Death pushed him away.

"Sergius is the first of Death's Reapers," Constantine told Nico. "Please have a seat before you pass out."

"What's a Reaper, and can I be one?" Nico stared at Sergius like a thirsty man eyeing at water.

"You have no idea what it is and you want to be one. What is wrong with you boy?" Constantine slapped Nico over the head.

"Sergius is huge." Nico pointed at his friend. "We could get Marie back and beat those bloodsuckers. I'm in. So what's a Reaper?"

"Our future Army of super humans," Death announced. "Now I'm going to put this one to bed before he falls on his face."

"But we have to find Marie," Sergius protested.

Death picked him up in his arms like a small child and headed out of the room.

"It sounds like we know exactly where Marie is," Death told Sergius, who was struggling to keep his head up. "Unless you rest and let the transformation take effect, you will be useless to her and us. Now sleep."

With that command, Sergius passed out in Death's arms. "Constantine, I'll be right back."

Death walked out of the room with Sergius. Nico's mouth was still open and Constantine tapped it with his paws.

"Nico, breathe," Constantine told him.

"Can I be a Reaper?" Nico whispered to Constantine.

"That is up to Death to decide, but tell me everything the message said." Constantine sat on the table and faced Nico.

"That the vampires had Marie, and if we wanted to see her,

we needed to be at the port by dusk tomorrow," Nico repeated the message a lot slower this time.

"Anything else?" Constantine asked.

"No, but you know it's a trap. They are planning to kill us." Nico fidgeted in his chair.

"Sounds like we are going to have a long day ahead of us."

Death entered the room. "Constantine, we need to scout that location and figure out any potential places we could be attacked. Nico, you need stay here with Sergius."

"Are you going to make me into a Reaper?" Nico asked Death.

"Not until we find out the full extent of his powers," Death replied. "It doesn't do us any good to have a muscular Sergius with no extra strength."

"Finally you are speaking reason here." Constantine hopped off the table, waving his tail. "We might as well get started, and you have souls to collect as well."

"Yes, my job is never done," Death replied.

"Nico, if anyone comes in the house, hide," Constantine ordered him.

Nico nodded and headed towards Sergius' room. Constantine waited for him to leave the room before jumping out the window.

"And I'm the dramatic one here," Death told himself and vanished through the door.

CHAPTER NINE

The stars lined the sky, making the march to the port a less somber occasion. The streets were packed with pedestrians. It appeared the residents knew of the meeting with the vampires and avoided eye contact. Some closed their doors and windows when Constantine and Sergius walked by. Sergius had convinced Nico and Linus to stay behind. With their current human condition, the only thing both of them would achieve was death. Constantine led the way down the main road. As they plotted their route, he explained to Sergius there was no need to hide since the vampires were expecting them.

It didn't take Constantine and Sergius long to reach the port. There were no ships by the pier the vampires selected. The port was empty, at least of humans. Constantine sniffed the air and his tail stood up straight.

"What is it?" Sergius asked, keeping his features as neutral as possible.

"We have company, at least six of them," Constantine replied through gritted teeth.

"I can hear them," Sergius told him.

Constantine snapped his head up and looked at Sergius. "Anything else you can do that you haven't told me?"

A small smile spread across Sergius' face. "I can see perfectly clear in the night. I have never seen so many details in my life."

"Let's hope this means you won't be surprised from behind." Constantine turned to face away from the water as four vampires descended from the sky. "I wondered if they can truly fly or just jump really high."

"I don't think it matters because we are still outnumbered." Sergius turned to face the group who were all wearing hoods that covered their faces.

"We didn't think you would come, and instead you show up

alone? How brave," a tall vampire with a brown cape and a hood told Sergius as he walked closer to them. "Allow me to introduce myself. I'm Anthony."

"Why do we care?" Constantine growled. "Besides, if you are so brave, why don't you show us your face?"

"All in due time. I figured it would be a shame for you to die today without knowing the name of the person that killed you." Anthony took a bow and his companions laughed.

"How nice of you. Where is Marie?" Sergius shouted, his eyes scanning the crowd.

"Oh, she is here, but we wanted to give you one last chance." Anthony pointed at his companions with his elongated nails.

"One last chance for what?" Sergius asked, crossing his arms over his chest.

"To join us," Anthony purred to them. "You will not win this war, so join us and live forever."

"Unfortunately, we have already pledged our allegiance to one powerful being, and he doesn't share very well." Constantine squared his shoulders and showed the vampires his own teeth. "Give us the girl and we can make this a short night."

"You had your chance. Don't say we didn't warn you." Anthony waved behind him and two more vampires dragged a small female between them.

Marie was bound by her wrists and legs. Her head was covered by a piece of cloth and her toga was ripped and filthy. Her body was exposed in different places, making Sergius growl in anger. Constantine held him back as the vampires dragged the poor girl in front of them.

"Marie, is that you? Speak to me?" Sergius asked, his voice quivering.

"Sergius, oh please do as they say," Marie whimpered.

"Something is not right," Constantine whispered to Sergius.

"What?" Sergius looked quickly down at him.

"Can't you smell it? She is not right?" Constantine sniffed the air again.

Sergius stepped back and took a deep breath. He looked around at the vampires again.

"I can't tell the difference. There are too many of them," Sergius replied, looking around.

"Take the cover off her head," Constantine ordered.

"You don't trust us?" Anthony placed his hand over his heart.

"Not in a thousand years, and I've lived that long. Now!" Constantine shouted.

Anthony signaled for one of the guards holding Marie to take the cloth away. Marie looked at the ground with her eyes closed. While her toga was dirty and ripped, her face was clean and almost glistening. Her complexion sparkled in the night and she had a glow about her. Sergius made his way slowly towards Marie.

"No!" Constantine growled. "She's been turned."

"What?" Sergius stopped to look at Constantine.

"Aren't you the smart little cat now?" Marie told Constantine as she raised her face to look at them.

Sergius screamed as he looked at Marie. "Oh God, what are you?"

"I could say the same thing about you, my little Sergius," Marie told him as she met his eyes.

Marie strolled seductively towards Sergius with her hips moving to their own beat. She ripped the remains of her top off, exposing her breasts and caressing them gently.

"Don't you want me, Sergius?" Marie flashed a bewitching grin while she removed the remainder of her clothing.

"You are not Marie. Stay way." Sergius stumbled backwards.

Marie flew on him and pinned him down, her face pressing closer as she tried to kiss him, but Sergius elbowed her aside. He rolled to his feet and Constantine joined him.

"You can see them for what they really are, right?" Constantine asked, extending all his claws.

Sergius swallowed his own saliva before talking. "I don't know what she is. It's like a bat and a shark had a baby and created a monster. Her breath is like hot, rotten carcass burning your flesh."

"That is no way to talk about a lady, Sergius." Marie laughed at him and joined her fellow vampires.

"Oh God, it's Marie. She must still be in there." Sergius moved in her direction but Constantine pulled him back.

"She is gone," Constantine whispered.

"I can't see the monster anymore." Sergius watched as Marie covered herself with a hood similar to her companions.

"Different," Constantine said.

"What is it?" Sergius asked, looking around as six vampires

made a semi-circle around them.

"No time for explanations now, but can you smell them?" Constantine angled himself towards the vampires approaching on the right-hand side.

"Unfortunately yes." Sergius faced the left side.

"Sergius, why do you always have to be difficult? We could have been together forever," Marie told him, shaking her head.

"You have made your choice. What a pity," Anthony announced. "When Death comes to collect your souls, give him a message. His time has passed and we are running this world now."

Marie wrapped her arms around Anthony and waved at Sergius and Constantine. The six vampires moved all at once and attacked Sergius and Constantine. Constantine was prepared for the attack and hurdled over the assailants. He flipped his body in midair and landed on the back of one of the vampires. Before the vampire could react, Constantine decapitated the man with his claws, and they exploded into a cloud of dust.

Sergius was not having the same luck as Constantine. He was stuck in a hand to hand battle with two vampires who were a lot better at fighting than he was. While Sergius' new-found speed allowed him to block the vampires' punches, it didn't help him fight back very well. He managed to kick one of the vampires hard enough to crack a wall with his landing. Unfortunately, the blow was not fatal, and the vampires kept coming. Constantine had taken three of the vampires down by the time he made it to Sergius. One of Sergius' attackers had acquired a knife and was ready to stab Sergius when Death appeared.

"Three against one is not a fair fight," Death announced as he ripped off the head of the vampire.

Death crossed the cloud of dust that was left from the vampire and threw a scythe at Sergius, who managed to catch it in midair. With two quick swings, Sergius dispatched one of his vampires. Constantine took care of the remaining one, leaving Death to wipe dust off his clothes.

"I understand the concept, dust to dust, but do they need to have that much of it?" Death asked, shaking dust out of his hair.

"The horror! Vampire ashes in your hair," Constantine mocked.

"I don't see you cleaning yourself off with your tongue now." Death pointed at Constantine's back, which was covered in dust.

"Ick." Constantine gave himself a brisk shake, trying to knock away as much of the dust as possible. "Fine, you do have a point. This country is nasty enough without adding dead vampires to my list of things to clean. Do you know how long it takes me to get clean? I'm not licking dead corpses off me."

"Now that we settled our priorities, are you okay?" Death asked Sergius.

"They turned her," Sergius mumbled.

"That was to be expected, but I'm sorry," Death told him, patting him on the back.

"Good news, he can smell them," Constantine reported to Death.

"Can he see them?" Death asked.

"You two know I'm standing right here," Sergius interrupted, but they ignored him.

"Yes but only when they make eye contact." Constantine looked at Sergius again.

"About that, why?" Sergius leaned on his scythe.

"The eyes are the windows to the soul, and they don't have one," Death clarified. "You see what is left behind, the monster that destroyed the human soul."

"Well, I would be perfectly fine if I never saw that again," Sergius announced.

"Too late for that, my little apprentice," Death shattered Sergius' dream, making his head droop. "Word is going to spread now that they know you can see them. They will be looking for you."

"It's not like they stopped looking," Sergius replied, and Constantine agreed. "Now what?"

"Now we train," Constantine jumped in.

"Train?" Sergius asked.

"Just because you have superhuman powers doesn't mean you know how to use them." Constantine walked in circles around Sergius. "You are terrible in a fight, and that will get you killed."

"Constantine is right. You need training." Death cracked his knuckles as he looked towards the ocean. "We also need to increase our numbers. This is going to be a nasty war."

"Of course it is," Constantine replied, wiping dust off his face. "This stuff is nasty. Are you heading back with us?"

"No, I have deliveries," Death said softly. "Can you two make it without me?"

"Of course we can," Constantine replied, rolling his eyes. "It's time to test how fast our little Reaper is."

"We can?" Sergius squealed.

"He is all yours," Death told Constantine, covering his face.

"Yes, we can. You are a strange boy," Constantine told Sergius who was bouncing on the balls of his feet with excitement. "Now, pay attention. We are going to cross the city at a very fast pace. Stick close to me and don't pass me. Got it?"

"Yes, sir." Sergius gave Constantine a salute.

"Please try not to kill him," Death told Constantine before disappearing.

"Ready, let's go." Constantine took off at a full sprint without waiting for a reply from Sergius. Within a few seconds, Sergius was running right behind Constantine and keeping up with him. A devious grin appeared on Constantine's face as he sped up.

CHAPTER TEN

PRESENT DAY- NEW BOSTON ROAD TEXARKANA

Constantine took a deep breath and settled himself in the seat. Bob waited patiently looking out of his window.

"Boss, are you seeing what I'm seeing?" Bob pointed towards the small outdoor plaza in front of Oaklawd Village.

The shops were closed this late in the night, but Bob and Constantine could see a group of seven teenagers hovering on the sidewalk. The group stood in a semi-circle facing the buildings.

"It looks like Shorty's dealer has migrated to this side of the street." Constantine leaned out the window. "Why don't we pay this little group a visit?"

Before Bob could say a word, Constantine hopped out of the window and was maneuvering his way towards the group. Bob grabbed a few syringes from the truck's console. By the time Bob made it out of the truck, Constantine was nowhere to be seen. Bob untucked his shirt, messed up his hair, and limped towards the group. Some of the teens noticed Bob, but they dismissed him.

As Bob neared, the teens in the middle of the group floated off the ground. He looked around the parking lot and across the street. No other human was anywhere in sight. From the small of his back, Bob pulled out his dart gun.

"Those are some dangerous drugs you are playing with," Bob told the group in a soft voice.

"Who asked you, old man?" the tallest of the group shouted.

Bob covered the distance between himself and the group in less than three seconds. When the youth turned to confront Bob, he had the dart-gun pointed at his face. The teen screamed. Some members of his group tried to run away, but he hit two right in the back with tranquilizers, knocking them to the ground immediately.

"I recommend not running. The pavement leaves a nasty mark when you land," Bob told the teens, and his words stopped the others from trying to escape. "Hand me the pixie dust."

"We don't know what you are taking about," the tall boy replied.

"Really?" Bob walked over to the two floating teens. "You are telling me this is happening from thinking happy thoughts?"

Bob grabbed one of the floaters—a red-headed girl—and injected her with the syringe. The girl gasped for air and dropped to the ground. Her friends rushed to her side and helped her up, as Bob administered the second antidote to their floating companion.

"You know this stuff causes brain damage, seizures, and even strokes, right?" Bob asked as he examined the pupils of the red-headed girl. "Prolonged exposure to this stuff will kill you."

"Aren't you supposed to say *can* kill us?" the tall one asked.

"There is no *can* or *may*. It will kill you. Just a matter of time." Bob flashed a light in the pupils of the young man who was not responding. "Another three minutes and you will be wiping the drool of your friend for the rest of his life. He has enough dust in him to turn him into a vegetable."

Bob pulled his cell out. The teens rushed towards their friend, who now laid unconscious on the ground. The red-head cried on his shoulder, her back heaving uncontrollably.

"Shorty, I need you to swing by with the truck. I have a kid who needs medical attention now." Bob waited, listening to Shorty's quick reply, then he hung up.

"Guess what I found?" Constantine asked, emerging from behind the building and dragging a male pixie by his wings.

"Let me go." The outraged pixie thrashed as Constantine slapped him on the ground with his paws. "If you damage my wings I'm going to report you at Reapers."

"Perfect, I'll save you the trip," Constantine hissed. "I'm the top feline in charge, report."

"Oh God, no!" The pixie howled. "Constantine, I'm so sorry. I didn't recognize you."

"You didn't recognize me? What?" Constantine growled, spraying spit all over the pixie. "How many talking cats do you know in Texarkana? One! There is only one. Me, Constantine, feline extraordinaire."

"I think I'm suffering from brain damage. I hear the cat

talking." The red head covered her head and rocked back and forth.

"Explain to me how these kids can buy crap from a six-inch pixie, but they are shocked by a talking cat? How does that work?" Constantine slapped the pixie one more time for extra emphasis.

"It's because I'm cute," the pixie answered from the ground.

"Cuteness is not going to get you out of this," Constantine told the pixie, only inches away from his face. "You know the rules. It is illegal to sell dust, magic, or any other concoctions to minors."

"Minors? They are minors? I just thought they were really short humans," the pixie rambled.

"Don't be ridiculous. I would rip your wings off with my bare teeth if they didn't taste so bad." Constantine whacked the pixie over the head.

"This is police brutality. I'm going to report you." The pixie covered his face with his hands before Constantine could hit him again.

"To whom? Do you want to talk to Death? I'm sure we can make an appointment for you." Bob told the pixie as he leaned down to look at him.

"Death? No way," the pixie screamed. "Don't you have a complaints department?"

"You are looking at it," Constantine told the pixie. "You are going downtown. A week at the station should help you remember the rules and regulations of Haven."

"You are going to take him to the police station?" The tall teen shaky voice showed exactly how nervous he was.

"Not the human jail, but our Union Station," Constantine replied with a wink.

"The old train station? Why?" This time the tall teen sounded more confident, his tone strong and sure.

"Let's just say it's under new management and for a whole new purpose. Look, Shorty is here, so I recommend everyone clear the area." Constantine dove out of the way, dragging the pixie with him.

Bob pulled the red-head with him, while knocking the two boys away from the sidewalk just as Shorty made a classic stop in front of them. He stopped inches away from the comatose teen on the ground. The three teens that were standing jumped at Bob, and the tall boy's fists were shaking.

"What is wrong with you people?" screamed the tall boy.

"This is coming from the boy snorting pixie dust." Bob shook his head.

"Shorty, do you still have the cage?" Constantine held the pixie by his wings in front of him.

"Of course, Boss. What do we have?" Shorty ran to the bed of the truck and grabbed a small cage similar to those used for catching squirrels.

"Your dealer." Constantine handed Shorty the pixie.

"You little bastard," Shorty yelled at the pixie. "You had me running up and down New Boston Road chasing your little trail. You are going on ice for this."

"You really don't mean that, do you?" The pixie's voice broke, and Shorty slammed him in the cage.

"Oh yes I do. We have an industrial-sized fridge with a two-by-four block of ice that you will be sitting on for a week." Shorty glared at his prisoner.

"Shorty, no cruel and unusual punishments. The sentence must match the crime," Bob lectured his old friend.

"Fine, a day in the fridge and the rest in the basement." Shorty stuck his tongue out at the pixie and put him in the truck. "Okay, who needs medical attention?"

"They all need to be examined, but that one on the floor and the red-head need their stomachs pumped," Bob ordered. "Everyone in the back of the truck, now."

The tall teen tried to protest but Shorty and Bob both pointed guns at his face. Tall and his quiet companion helped the red head into the truck. Bob and Shorty dragged the other three knocked-out boys to the truck. Once everyone was loaded inside, Shorty peeled out of the parking lot, heading towards downtown.

"I hate to admit it, but Isis is right. Shorty is a menace to society in that truck," Constantine announced, watching Shorty burn rubber down the road.

"You gave him the truck," Bob told his boss.

"Not one of my brightest ideas, but he does get to places faster now." Constantine laughed at his own joke and Bob joined in.

"Do you think we scared away our little werewolves?" Bob asked as they marched back to the truck.

"We are not that lucky, my friend." Constantine reached the truck first and leap back in through the window.

Bob made himself comfortable in the driver's seat and went

back to scanning the area. The drive-thru line at Whataburger was still as long as when they'd left. Cars continued to arrive at the location.

"This is one busy place," Bob said, leaning against his window.

"It's all about convenience, Not many places are open twenty-four hours in Texarkana," Constantine replied. "Some of our night creatures are taking full advantage. I'm surprised a few of them haven't opened any late-night establishments."

"I heard Abuelita is planning to extend her hours to accommodate the late crowd," Bob told Constantine.

"That is the best news ever! Mexican food available during our stake-outs? She needs to hurry." Constantine licked his lips and rolled in his seat.

Bob laughed. "So boss, what happened to your vampire war? I have a feeling it doesn't end there."

"I wish that was the end, and we had a happily ever after." Constantine sat back up in the seat. "The battles raged on from town to town. Death was really good at making Reapers, but for every one we made, they raised fifty vampires. Our numbers were dwindling, and we were becoming less selected in our transformation process. We needed more bodies. Those were dark times, but we didn't realize they were only the beginning."

CHAPTER ELEVEN

LATE SUMMER 476 AD- ROME

The smell of burned flesh was thick in the air. Dawn was only a few hours away, but the vampires kept fighting like it was merely sunset. Constantine had three pinned against a wall. They were recently made, still clumsy and struggling to master their full powers. Hunger moved most of the new ones to action, and the smell of spilled blood drove them nuts. After five months of fighting, Sergius was an expert at decapitations. With only a single swing, vampires' heads rolled and bodies crumpled to dust.

The fighting was brutal that night. The Reapers had decided to change their plans and went on a full-scale assault. Their first target was a large residence in the center of the city. Based on their informants, one of the wealthy citizens was aiding the vampires and allowing them to stay at his home. Upon their arrival in the house, they found that the citizen wasn't aiding the vampires…he was one of them.

"Constantine, they are heading underground. We won't be able to fight them there," Julius yelled from the second floor.

"We have three Reapers down." Sergius tossed one of the injured Reaper over his shoulder and dragged the other two. "We need to get out of here."

"Torch the place," Constantine ordered after ripping apart his three vampires. "Set up a perimeter around the house. Cut down anyone trying to escape."

"On my way." Julius ran to the first oil lamp near the stairs and lit the curtains on fire.

He whistled across the house and Reapers scattered through doors and windows, each one knocking candles and lamps down on their way out. Constantine helped Sergius drag the injured Reapers out of the house. Over twenty Reapers, all covered in blood and bruises, surrounded the house, waiting for their enemy to appear.

Julius was the last one to leave the house.

"How many vampires were left?" Constantine asked Julius as he reached them.

"At least twenty in the cellar." Julius dropped on the ground next to one of the wounded Reapers. "What do you need me to do?"

"Stop the bleeding on Amos's arm." Sergius pointed to the unconscious Reaper next to Julius. "As long as the bleeding stops, he will be able to heal himself."

"How bad is Lucas?" Julius asked, holding Amos's arm with one hand and ripping a piece of his clothes with the other.

"Not as bad as he looks." Constantine smelled the wound on Lucas' shoulder. "His muscles are already healing themselves. He will be back to normal in three days, but we need to cover this wound."

"Let me finish here and I will take care of that." Sergius finished bandaging the leg of the Reaper he was carrying.

"Fangs on the roof!" a Reaper shouted from the left flank.

"Don't follow," Constantine ordered.

"We are not taking him out?" Julius glanced over his shoulder at the crouching figure on the roof.

"If you said twenty are still in that house, the one on the roof is just a distraction." Constantine pointed to the right side where four figures were sneaking out a window. "Any questions?"

"On my way." Julius pulled two small daggers from his pants and sprinted across the grounds.

Three more Reapers followed him as silent as the night. Before the vampires could assess the situation, the Reapers were on them. Julius decapitated the first one using both of his knives. His companions speared the other with their scythe, and the vampires were dispatched in record time. Julius ripped another piece of his clothing off and crept to the open window in the lower level. He lit the material on fire and threw it down the lower window. The flame quickly spread and screams erupted from the lower levels. Within minutes, a slew of vampires were rushing out the building.

Reapers attacked from all sides of the house. The vampires trying to escape the house were experienced fighters, which made the battle more intense and dangerous. A few of the Reapers were knocked down, others were cut, and some tossed yards away.

Sergius joined the battle after bandaging his companions.

"Nico, guard these three!" Constantine shouted as he ran to

the battle. "Don't let any of those blood suckers near them."

"Not a problem." Nico position himself in the center of the bodies and spun his scythe with expert precision.

A vampire escaped the front line of Reapers, knocking two of them out. He headed for Sergius, who was busy battling two other vampires by himself. Claws extended and fangs bared, the vampire flew to take his kill shot. In mid-air, Constantine intercepted him bringing him out of the air with his feline power. The vampire and Constantine rolled on the ground several times, each trying to gain an advantage over the other. Constantine's tail wrapped around the vampire's leg, pulling his attention away long enough for Constantine to find an opening. Before the vampire could react, Constantine ripped his neck off.

From the cloud of dust, Constantine emerged to dispatch two other vampires trying to escape. The vampire on the roof blew a loud horn but nothing happened. As the last note left the instrument, the first rays of sunlight broke through the night. The vampires screamed in agony as the sunlight engulfed them, tearing them to shreds. The Reapers stepped away to give the sun room to finish its work.

"This was part of your plan, right?" Sergius asked Constantine, holding a Scythe he picked up from one of his peers.

"Of course," Constantine answered, not looking at Sergius.

"Right." Sergius laughed. "What did you think the alarm was for? A retreat or back-up?"

"That is a very good question. Too bad we won't be finding that out today." Constantine rubbed his paw on Sergius' clothes.

"Do you really have to clean yourself on me?" Sergius asked, pulling his blood-covered clothes away from Constantine.

"I'm not licking vampires' dust. That is disgusting." Constantine gave himself a brisk shake, scattering dust everywhere. "Besides, you are already dirty."

"Have you considered wearing clothes to avoid the dust and blood on your fur?" Julius asked, joining Sergius and Constantine.

"Please tell me he was hit in the head and lost his mind." Constantine pointed at Julius with his claws. "Can you possibly imagine covering this amazing coat with that?"

"At least your coat wouldn't be getting dirty all the time," Sergius added with a shrug.

"What side are you on?" Constantine rolled his eyes and

marched back to Nico.

"I'm sure we can get a toga in your size," Julius teased as he followed closely behind Constantine.

"Nico, give me some good news before I have to choke these two." Constantine sat down next to the unconscious Reapers.

"Nothing good." Nico pulled out two parchments from his clothes, handing them to Sergius.

Sergius unrolled the parchment and spread them on the ground in front of Constantine.

"This can't be right. These documents are addressed to the Emperor." Sergius scanned the documents several times, reading to himself.

"We knew this could be a possibility. It makes sense," Constantine told the group. "Who else could control the Legions?"

"What you are implying is that the Emperor of Rome is a vampire? That is impossible." Julius threw his hands in the air and paced around the bodies.

"Constantine, we can't win a battle against Rome. We are barely holding on now." Sergius covered his face with his hands in resignation.

"Alone, no. They would wipe us all out," Constantine told the men.

"I don't like that tone in your voice," Nico told Constantine, glancing at Sergius and Julius for support.

"What are you talking about?" Constantine replied, his eyes big and innocent.

"That one that says we are in serious trouble." Nico pointed directly at Constantine.

"There is only one way to end this war. We need to cut off the head of the snake," Constantine announced.

"By the Gods! We are all going to die a horrible death," Julius added, taking deep breaths.

"What do you have in mind?" Sergius asked, sitting next to Constantine.

"You have gone mad just like him," Julius shouted.

"I have some friends outside the border that have been waiting for an opportunity for payback. It's time for us to join forces." Constantine smiled.

"What kind of friends?" Sergius leaned in closer to Constantine.

"Some called them Barbarians, but they are a really nice group of people," Constantine replied in a sweet voice.

"Yes, if the Emperor doesn't kill us, the barbarians will." Julius stopped fidgeting and sat on the ground next to Constantine. "Just tell us your plan. At least if we die, we will see it coming that way."

"I'm starting to think being dramatic is contagious." Constantine looked deep in Julius's eyes. "You get that from Death. I'm positive."

"Very funny," Julius answered, poking Constantine on the side of his ribs.

"Stop that." Constantine giggled. "Everyone focus. Julius, we need you to continue the attacks on the vampires. We don't want them to realize anything has changed. Sergius and I will be traveling to meet my friends at sea and coordinate an attack."

"Sailing is going to take forever. Why don't you ask Death to take you there? We don't have a lot of time." Nico waved his hands in front of him.

"Hard to convince people to help you when Death is at your side," Constantine explained.

"That is true," Julius conceded. "Fine, you two head out to find the barbarians. We will continue to cause trouble for our dear friends. When do you leave?"

"As soon as Sergius gets cleaned up." Constantine stood up and Sergius followed.

"Julius, are you going to be able to handle everything while we are gone?" Sergius faced his friend.

"Believe it or not, creating a little chaos is my specialty." Julius gave them both a wicked grin.

"That is what I'm afraid of." Constantine patted Julius's leg. "Don't burn the city down before we return. Sergius, we need to hurry. I know a guy who can give us a lift. And Julius. Take good care of them."

Constantine took another look at the Reapers and his eyes shone with unshed tears right before he took off down the road.

"We will be back as soon as possible." Sergius extended his hand to Julius, but he swiped it away and hugged him instead.

"Try not to let that silly fur-ball get you killed," Julius whispered in Sergius' ear.

"I will do my best, and you do the same." Sergius gave Julius another hug.

Sergius hugged Nico and kissed both of his cheeks. Nico was ready to cry, but somehow Sergius pulled away and followed after Constantine. He never looked back to say goodbye to his friends. Instead, he rushed down the quiet streets in the early hours of the morning, enjoying the rays of sun.

At least the sun was part of their team.

CHAPTER TWELVE

Constantine and Sergius approached a large ship off the coast of Italy. Their small vessel moved swiftly through the waters without making a sound. Their captain was covered in a dark wool robe from head to toe.

"Boatman, you have made incredible time," Constantine praised the captain.

"How did you pull that off?" Sergius asked, looking around the empty ship.

"I have my ways, little brother," the Boatman replied in a scratchy tone.

"Do I want to know what is underneath the robe?" Sergius whispered to Constantine.

"No, unless you are ready to take your final ride." Constantine moved closer to the Boatman as he maneuvered his vessel towards the battleship.

"Are you sure this is safe?" the Boatman asked, examining his surroundings.

"I sent word, so Sunigilda is expecting us." Constantine pointed towards the side of the ship where a rope ladder was hanging.

"You know that woman is trouble." The Boatman directed his ship smoothly towards the ladder.

"Have you met any human who isn't trouble?" Constantine replied.

"You are so right." The Boatman laughed.

"You two remember I'm still standing right here?" Sergius asked them.

The Boatman and Constantine both spun around to look at Sergius. Constantine's eyes glowed red in the moonlight, and so did Boatman's. Sergius cringed and strolled away in the direction of the ladder.

"Never mind, you both can go back to facing the other way."

Sergius grabbed his bag and examined the edge of the boat. "Are you ready, Constantine?"

"As ready as we are going to get." Constantine leaped on Sergius' back and wrapped around his neck. "Boatman, we shouldn't be long."

"I will be here waiting. The boss is handling the souls alone tonight." The Boatman took a seat and made himself comfortable.

Sergius gave the Boatman one last look before starting to climb, and he was scratching his face with a white skeleton hand. Sergius snapped his head back to the front and climbed the ladder, not attempting to look back. At the deck of the ship, a beautiful woman waited for them.

"What took you so long?" The woman glanced around the deck, rubbing her hands on her tunic and glancing over her shoulder.

"Sorry Sunigilda, we came as quickly as possible, but it is a little hard to judge time when you are riding the ship of the dead," Constantine replied sarcastically, jumping off Sergius. "Just take us to your husband."

"Follow me and hurry." Sunigilda wrapped herself with her blanket and led the way towards the inside of the ship.

Soldiers moved out of her way while their eyes remained locked on both Sergius and Constantine. Sergius kept his head down and stayed close to Sunigilda, and soon, she knocked at a wooden door on the far side.

"My husband, it is me," Sunigilda announced.

A large soldier with long hair and a full beard opened the door. He allowed Sunigilda to enter but blocked the door for Sergius and Constantine.

"They are with me," Sunigilda told the soldier.

"We don't allow strangers near the General without proper inspection." The soldier approached Sergius.

"We don't have time for this." Constantine walked underneath the soldiers legs and entered the cabin.

"By God, what kind of sorcery is this?" The soldier spun around to face Constantine.

All four people in the cabin stood up and pulled out their swords.

"Oh, everyone relax. If I wanted to hurt you, you would all be dead by now," Constantine told the group, jumping on the table attached to the wall.

"Odoacer, this is Constantine." Sunigilda rushed to her husband's side.

"Woman, what kind of witchcraft have you brought upon us?" Odoacer, a large man with a mustache, asked his wife.

"General, I told you it was bad luck to have a woman on board." The first soldier pointed his sword at Constantine.

"Constantine is the messenger of Death," Sunigilda explained.

"That is definitely not helping us," Sergius muttered from the door.

"Are you plotting to kill me?" Odoacer grabbed his wife by the throat.

"Not you, barbarian. Let her go," Constantine told him casually, making himself comfortable at the table. "We have a mutual enemy."

"Who could we possibly have in common?" Odoacer released his wife and faced Constantine.

"Orestes." Constantine licked his paws as the name settled over the room.

"Orestes?" Sergius was the first one to speak. "I thought we wanted Augustus dead."

"The boy Emperor is only a figure head placed there by his father. The real power is Orestes." Constantine directed his full attention towards Odoacer. "Unless you have made peace with his double crossing last year and denying you the lands that he promised."

"You are very well informed for a cat." Odoacer put his sword away and the rest of his troops followed.

"I make it my business to stay very well informed." Constantine took on his Sphinx pose.

"What has the great General Orestes done to you?" Odoacer took a seat near the wall, while his men flanked the table.

"We have reasons to believe the great General is a bloodsucker." Constantine stood on the table.

"A vampire!" one of the soldiers shouted.

"Is that so hard to believe?" Constantine asked the man.

"It actually makes sense," Odoacer added. "I couldn't figure out how he was always one step ahead of us. His power continued to expand, but his spies were always more lethal at night. What are you proposing?"

"A coordinated assault to take place in three weeks." Constantine signaled Sergius to come over.

Sergius pulled out several maps from his toga and spread them out next to Constantine.

"We have been monitoring his movements and if we attack Rome at the same time, we should be able to force him out." Constantine drew a line with his claws on the first map.

"What do we get from helping you?" Odoacer asked, walking to the table to look at the maps.

"Italy and the empire." Constantine hovered over the map where Italy was located.

"You are giving me the entire empire? So what do you two get?" Odoacer played with his mustache as he looked at the map.

"Freedom from those creatures." Constantine moved away from the map, giving Odoacer room.

"This seems too good to be true." Odoacer moved to his chair and sat down.

"We are very well compensated by our employer," Constantine said, looking back at Sergius, who nodded in agreement. "Besides Flavius Odoacer, King of Italy, has a nice ring to it."

"King of Italy," Odoacer repeated the title in a whisper.

"That is a great title," Sunigilda supplied.

"I will be king and my army would finally have the land they were promised, and you get a bunch of dead vampires. Sounds like we are getting the better end of this deal." Odoacer crossed his legs together and leaned back in his chair.

"Sounds like you shouldn't pass on this offer," Constantine told Odoacer, wiping his face with his paws.

"Fine, but if we are betrayed again, you are going to find yourself wishing Death *would* take you away." Odoacer pulled a dagger from an inside pocket of his jacket and tossed it next to Constantine.

"If you are trying to intimidate us, don't waste your time." Constantine slowly lowered his paws. "I'm over two-thousand years old, and I have done things you couldn't even imagine in your worst nightmares."

"Sounds like we are understanding each other." Odoacer smiled broadly at both Sergius and Constantine. "What is your plan?"

"In three weeks, we coordinate an attack on the city that

would force the general out of hiding," Constantine said softly. "We need to get him away from the Emperor and his troops."

"That is it?" the first soldier asked.

"We have found simplicity works best every time." Constantine winked.

"Simple but brutal...I like it," Odoacer proclaimed to his soldiers. "Aulas, it seems we will be changing course again."

"As you wish, my general." Aulas saluted Odoacer and headed out of the cabin.

"Sergius, please give the last documents to our new allies." Sergius followed Constantine's request and provided two rolls of parchment to Odoacer. "There is the location of our forces and details of the enemy. On August twenty-second, we will be in a position to charge the castle. We will need you and your men to attack the legions all around the capital. Can you handle that?"

"We are trained soldiers," Odoacer answered.

"Perfect, don't be late," Constantine told the man as he hopped down from the table. "We have things to do."

Sergius followed Constantine out of the cabin and to the upper deck. They made it to the top floor in silence.

"Do you think this is going to work?" Sergius asked as they reached the edge of the ship where the ladder was located.

"Revenge is a powerful motivator, so yes, it will work." Constantine leaped on Sergius' back and once again wrapped himself around his neck. "Now we just need to make sure the Reapers are ready for the upcoming battle."

"They will be ready. For now, we need to concentrate on getting down from here." Sergius dove over the edge of the boat and landed smoothly in the Boatman's ship.

"Now you are just showing off," Constantine muttered.

"Not bad timing, fur-man," the Boatman told Constantine.

"It was a simple proposal." Constantine bounced off Sergius and landed near the Boatman. "How quickly can you get us back to Rome?"

"Hold on tight, my friends. We are going to fly." The Boatman let out a long, eerie laugh that echoed even when he stopped.

"Sergius, hurry and get down here." Constantine dropped to the bottom of the boat beneath one of the wooden seats.

Sergius made it just as the Boatman picked up speed. Water

sprayed all around them as the boat cut through waves faster than the craft should be able to move. The Boatman sang to his own beat and moved the boat like he was the only one in the sea. Sergius held tight to the seat in front of him. Constantine, on the other hand, made himself comfortable on the floorboards and prepared himself to nap.

CHAPTER THIRTEEN

The team found out that three weeks was not a lot of time to mobilize an army, especially one that was half depleted. As Constantine and Sergius returned to Rome, they learned they had lost more than half of their Reapers. In an attempt to maintain their assaults and numbers, Death charged Julius the task of recruiting more candidates.

"Where exactly did you find these guys?" Constantine asked Julius for the tenth time in the last week.

"Our options were quite limited," Julius replied looking at two Reapers sparring with each other. "Most of our supporters were terrified once they learned we were going against the empire as well."

"I understand that, but these men are bloodthirsty." Constantine watched as one slammed his sparring partner against the ground. "Is he trying to kill him? He does know they are both on the same side?"

"I don't think so," whispered Sergius. "Are you planning to tell him?"

"I'm not getting near that mess in a thousand years," Constantine muttered back.

"By the way, what is wrong with their eyes?" Sergius pointed to three different Reapers walking by. "Why are they black instead of silver?"

"You noticed that too?" Julius leaned in. "Half of the new guys have eyes that way. The more ruthless they are, the darker the eyes."

"I don't like it." Constantine sniffed the air. "There is something off about them. I need to ask Death about it."

"It will need to wait until after the assault because we are attacking at dawn." Julius patted Sergius on the shoulder. "The fur-man might not need sleep, but you should get some. We only have a few hours before we move."

"I will," Sergius told Julius. "Constantine, the plan is going to work."

"It better work." Constantine turned his gaze to Sergius. "We have five-hundred Reapers scattered around the city waiting for dawn. You gave the orders?"

"Yes. Made sure they were repeated back at least five times." Sergius held out five fingers. "None of the civilians should be harmed but eliminate any and all vampires. What are you worried about?"

"I don't know," Constantine admitted.

"Julius is right. I need to get some rest before we head out." Sergius patted Constantine on the head, who in return swatted his hand away, laughing.

"It's going to be a brutal day," Constantine told himself as he marched to one of the windows to contemplate the stars.

Before the first rays of sunlight hit the earth, Reapers were in the position to attack the royal palace. They all wore long robes with hoods hiding their faces. Their scythes were sharpened to a fine point. Constantine watched the sky carefully from the rooftop of one of the nearby buildings.

"The madness ends tonight," Sergius told Constantine.

"I hope you are right," Constantine whispered.

As the sun broke through the clouds, Reapers descended on the palace. Some plummeted from rooftops as others ran across the streets. Sergius gave Constantine one last smile before dropping to the ground. Constantine watched the assault from his position, waiting for the first servants to be evacuated from the grounds. Instead of being escorted out, a Reaper chopped down two defenseless girls trying to leave.

"No!" Constantine growled.

"I created monsters," Death mumbled as he held on to the rooftop for support.

"I don't think you created them; we just gave them too much power." Constantine walked to the edge of the building. "We don't have a lot of time. Save the humans first, kill the vampires next, and take care of our mess later."

"You make it sound so simple, my old friend," Death told

him.

"Do you have a better plan?" Constantine looked back at Death as he prepared to pounce to the ground.

"Not at all." Death shook his head.

"In that case, we are going with mine. You take the right; I have the left." Constantine dove from the roof before Death could reply.

Constantine landed in the courtyard of the palace, but Death was already walking inside. The screams rattled through the palace from all directions. Constantine rushed inside, slamming into a dead body in the first corridor.

"Death walks the night," the soul told Constantine.

"Killers walk the night. Death is just a little too late tonight." Constantine ducked out of the way as an arm flew over his head. "This is a nightmare. Hey boy, listen to me."

The soul drifted in and out of awareness, looking down at his dead body. Constantine slapped his thigh, making the young man's gaze lock on him.

"Ouch, how did you do that?" The boy touched his thigh in astonishment.

"No time to explain, I need you to focus. Can you do that?" Constantine asked the young man, who nodded back. "Good. I need you to grab every soul you see and take them to the courtyard. Can you do that?"

"Soul?" The young man glanced around the corridor.

"Yes. Every soul, every ghost. I don't care what you call them. Can you get them out?" Constantine pointed at two more souls hovering over their dead bodies. "I need them out of here."

"What are we supposed to do in the courtyard?" the young man asked.

"Wait for Death to take you home," Constantine answered softly.

"Home." A smile spread across the young man's face. "Yes, I can do that."

Constantine did not have time to give him any more guidance because the young man ran to grab the first souls he could find. Constantine ran in the opposite direction towards the sounds of battle. He arrived in the throne room to find the place was a killing field. Blood covered the floors, the walls, and every living person in that room. A few vampires fought in a corner but most were fleeing down hallways. Constantine found Sergius in the center of the room, kneeling on the ground and completely covered in blood.

"Are you hurt?" Constantine shouted.

"Linus is dead." Sergius sobbed next to his dead friend.

"We will make them pay, Sergius." Constantine bared his teeth, ready to devour the enemy.

"It wasn't the vampires." Sergius closed Linus' eyes and forced himself to stand with his scythe. "Those Reapers killed him when he tried to save a young girl. They are killing everyone Constantine."

"This is worse than I expected." Constantine took a deep breath. "Sergius, I need you to get every human out of here. Can you do that for me?"

"What are you going to do?" Sergius asked, eyeing the carnage in the room.

"Stop them before everyone is dead." Constantine extended his claws. "Death is on the other side doing the same. They need to be stopped or they will kill Odoacer and his troops."

Constantine ran out of the room at a full sprint, moving with a vengeance. Every evil Reaper he found he cut down. Constantine followed the sound of metal crashing and found an underground chamber. Julius and ten of his men were fighting twenty vampires. The vampires were gaining ground and Reapers were being chopped down one at a time. Constantine leaped over the Reapers and landed on top of two vampires in full leopard form. The vampires were unable to reach the feast fast enough. In one fluid motion, Constantine ripped four of them apart. The Reapers took advantage of the confusion and rallied behind him.

They battled for almost an hour in the confined space, but eventually Constantine and the Reapers defeated the vampires. Only four Reapers were left standing, including Julius.

"I'm glad you made it, Constantine," Julius told the leopard. "That is you, right?"

"How many wild leopards have you seen in Rome lately?" Constantine asked Julius as he shifted back to his normal size.

"Leopards, none. I saw a few lions once, though." Julius wiped the blood from his face. "I think we lost him."

"Who?" Constantine asked.

"Who else? Orestes?" Julius replied, taking a knee.

"We will find him, but we have other problems now."

Constantine walked slowly towards Julius. "How many of those new Reapers have those black eyes?"

"What?" Julius mumbled.

"Almost a hundred, sir," one of the other Reapers replied.

"Are you sure?" Constantine marched over to the young man.

"Yes. Some of us have been monitoring them." He motioned with his head to his peers.

"There is something different about them, about the way they look at people." His friend moved closer to them.

"Constantine, what is going on?" Julius asked.

"They killed everyone they encountered, even our own," Constantine whispered.

"Are you sure?" Julius stood up very slowly.

"I saw it myself," Constantine told him.

"This is all my fault." Julius covered his face with his bloody hands. "I thought we needed fighters willing to do anything. I didn't know they would…"

"Constantine, Odoacer's troops have entered the city." Sergius rushed into the chamber. "Jesus Christ!"

"I know," Constantine replied. "We need to focus. Julius, Sergius, I need you two to take as many of our Reapers to meet Odoacer. He needs to secure the city and find Orestes as soon as possible. The rest of us need to find Augustus before our demented Reapers find him. Go."

"Constantine be careful," Sergius told him as he left the room.

"I'm sorry." Julius cried.

"You didn't do anything wrong, you couldn't see in the hearts of those monsters. Hurry, go." Constantine pushed Julius out the door. "You three follow them, and make sure you all come back."

"You are right. It is my fault." Death appeared behind Constantine.

"Ahh." Constantine jumped a few feet off the ground. "What is it with you sneaking around today? You are not even supposed to do that to me. I'm obviously exhausted if I'm not able to sense your arrival."

"There is too much death here for you to feel me properly." Death kneeled next to one of his Reapers. "I did this. I should have taken my time and inspected them better."

"Sure, there are hundreds of things we could have done better, but we didn't." Constantine slapped his friend over the head.

"Ouch." Death rubbed his head softly. "Have I mentioned you are violent?"

"Sometimes it's the only way to get you out of this doom state you get in," Constantine answered. "We don't have time to find who is at fault. We need to stop a hundred Reapers from killing half of Rome, destroy the remaining vampires, and put a barbarian on the throne. So can you focus now?"

"Are we doing the right thing?" Death asked Constantine.

"Only time will tell, but right now, we have work to do." Constantine pulled his old friend off the ground and dragged him outside. "You take these souls home, and I will find the soon-to-be former Emperor of Rome. Then we hunt some vampires. Simple enough?"

"You are nuts." Death forced a smile and wiped the tears from his cheeks. "Time to work."

Death disappeared down the hall and Constantine followed him. The morning was half way over but he was the best tracker in the empire. If anyone could save the young boy, he could.

CHAPTER FOURTEEN

PRESENT DAY- TEXARKANA

Bob sat in the truck, speechless. Constantine tapped the arm rest with his claws at a slow, steady beat. The silent stretched between them, and Constantine eventually faced Bob.

"Are you serious?" Bob had to swallow twice before the words could come out.

"The good news is, we saved Augustus," Constantine told Bob with a shrug. "Yes, he was deposed of the empire, and Odoacer's men declared him king. We did capture and kill Orestes in Placentia. Basically, everything was accomplished."

"Boss, you started the Dark Ages?" Bob mumbled as his eyes became increasingly bigger.

"One coup. It was one simple coup." Constantine stood up on his seat. "Do you know how many coups I had organized before that one? Do you know how many political powers I had dethroned? How was I supposed to know it was going to take humanity one-thousand years to get over that one?"

Bob busted into uncontrollable fits of laughter. "Humanities darkest time were instigated by you!"

"When people say it out loud, it always sounds a lot worse," Constantine mumbled, rolling his eyes.

"Did you at least kill off the vampires?" Bob struggled to breathe and speak at the same time.

"No!" Constantine pouted and sat back down. "It took us a year to hunt down all the demented Reapers. Julius didn't realize he had recruited blood-thirsty mercenaries. After we cleaned that mess, we spent the next seventy-seven years hunting down vampires in every part of the world. We didn't have time to focus on Rome. Both the East and the West of the Roman Empire had fallen into chaos. Our war only left more carnage in its wake."

"How did you stop the war?" Bob leaned closer to

Constantine, who was barely whispering.

"War," Constantine mumbled.

"War? What do you mean?" Bob asked.

"War intervened." Constantine almost choked on the words. "The great Horseman War mediated a treaty between Death and the Vampires."

"Now that is insane," Bob said incredulously.

"He had never mediated a successful peace treaty in his existence, and he was the one that ended the horror." Constantine covered his face with his paws. "To this day, I still have to hear about it. Of course, he took full advantage of the chaos and conducted some of his most memorable war campaigns against humanity, but he blames the Dark Ages on us."

"You technically started it," Bob added.

"Don't take his side," Constantine snapped.

"And Death?" Bob tried to change the topic a little.

"Damaged forever." Constantine took a deep breath. "That was the last time any human ever saw his real self. He blames himself for everything. Death became a monster to humanity, the bringer of suffering. To punish himself, he shifted to whatever vicious image a person believed Death was."

"Is he still punishing himself?" Bob asked.

"Not anymore. Now it's just a habit. At least that's what he wants me to believe." Constantine stared out the window with teary eyes.

"I'm sorry, boss." Bob reached over and touched Constantine on the back.

"Some lessons are hard to learn," Constantine admitted.

"What happened to the Reapers?" Bob asked softly.

"Asleep in the river Styx waiting for judgment day," Constantine gave Bob a weak smile.

"I. Need. Back up!" Isis's voice blared through the speaker system in the jeep.

Bob hit his head on the roof of the truck, startled by the sound. Constantine looked around the area for Isis.

"How in the hell did she find them before we did?" Constantine asked, his eyes still searching.

"It's Isis we are talking about. She would find trouble at a Tibetan Peace Summit." Bob pressed the speaker button on his truck.

"Isis where are you?" Bob asked.

"Behind Oaklawd Village," Isis mumbled back.

"Of course she is around the corner from us." Constantine shook his head. "Swing the truck around. I'll head that way now."

Constantine jumped out of the window again and dashed through the parking lot. Bob put the truck in drive and rushed after him.

"Never a dull moment," Bob told himself, shaking his head.

CONNECT WITH D. C. ONLINE:

For up to date promotions and release dates of upcoming books, sign up for the latest news here:

Author Page: www.dcgomez-author.com

www.bookbug.com/author-d-c-gomez

www.Facebook.com/dcgomez.author

www.Instagram.com/dc.gomez

www.goodreads.com/dcgomez

D.C. GOMEZ

ACKNOWLEDGMENTS

I would like to start by saying Thank You to each one of your for reading this book and being a part of this journey. Thank you so much for all the love and support you have given the Reaper team. A special thanks to all of Constantine's fans. The feline extraordinaire has changed my life as much as he changed Isis'. Thank you for opening your hearts to this special little family.

It takes a tribe to bring books to life. I'm so grateful for mine and their continuous support. Thank you to the amazing Mr. J. Patton Tidwell for taking on the challenge of being my super beta-reader for the Intern Diaries. Your comments and feedback are incredible. My heart goes out to my parents, brothers, sisters-in-law, and my better half. Thank you for understanding when I'm locked in the house writing. To my furry roommate, Chincha, thank you for keeping me sane during the late hours with treat-breaks.

To the talented and always patient Ms. Cassandra Fear, thank you for taking on the challenge of being my editor and cover designer. I couldn't have done this without you. To the amazing and patient Ms. Courtney Shockey, thank you so much for putting all the pieces together and giving me a beautiful book. Absolutely, it takes a village to get this done.

To all the dreamers in the world, never stop believing. The world needs your talent, your words, and your passion. Go forth and do amazing things.

ABOUT D. C. GOMEZ

D. C. Gomez was born in the Dominican Republic, but grew up in Salem, Massachusetts. She studied film and television at New York University. After college she joined the US Army, and proudly served for four years.

Those experiences shaped her quirky, and sometimes morbid, sense of humor. D.C. has a love for those who served and the families that support them. She currently lives in the quaint city of Wake Village, Texas, with her furry roommate, Chincha.

Made in the USA
Columbia, SC
26 July 2021